Blue York City

A.D. Rosa

Copyright © 2017 A.D. Rosa

All rights reserved.

ISBN:
ISBN- 9781521911235:

DEDICATED TO ALL MY LOVED ONES,
ESPECIALLY MY FAMILY.

Blue York City

*****

It was the dead of winter in all its usual and dreary doom. Gray skies were miles behind and ahead. New Years, and it started with the coldest day in a decade.

Outside the winds cut through every layer, and moaned as they flew through the streets and alleys, rattling our windows as they passed, bellowing like demons. The once pristine fallen white snow in the street mixed with dirt, plowed and shoveled to the corners and sides of the roads where it froze and slowly melted from brownish ugly mounds.

Everything was bleak except for the trees that lined our Brooklyn Street. They stood like tall shadows, with black swaying arms reaching in all directions. They were strong, beautiful, and made creaking sounds like horror movies. And, they waited, just like we did, for another chance to bloom after this near-death hibernation. People were saying it was the worst winter in a century. So much for global warming. I hoped it would taper and that there'd be some sun and warmth, if only briefly, but it didn't.

Sara and I sat on tiny stools at our little yellow table, trying not to look at each other while eating food that was as disappointing as the air between us. It broke us to eat condiment-topped meals, like this spaghetti and cheap tomato paste that tasted more like bad ketchup. But, we did it, because we had to.

The oven was open for heat. It was an old vintage one from the sixties or seventies that also had a side-heating vent. It sufficed. We used it constantly because we were always cold and stagnant, and we knew soon there would be no more of it. No more heat. No more oven. No more hot showers. No more lights. No more spaghetti or beans and rice to cook; just untoasted bread and cold soup, or whatever else could be eaten right from the can or package.

The electric and gas shut-off notices were piling up along with other unopened bills scattered somewhere within this mess. Bills and overdue notices were the only mail we got these days. We used the resources as we had them, and without a thought or care to cost or conservation because we knew we'd never settle them. It became our only feeling of simultaneous decadence and decency to have the place as hot as we could tolerate at all times, to take long steaming showers, and to leave lights on carelessly, or we would freeze from demoralization. We might freeze yet, slowly in clouds of our own breath in the dark. But as long as we had warmth and light we could pretend we had time, and we could pretend to forget.

I looked down at my plate, and with every bite my stomach shrunk from the lack of flavor, an all too familiar feeling. As much as I felt full from this slop, I also felt famished. Just one good meal could revive my will. The hunger for taste and texture, salt and fat, soft and sweet, roasted, baked, fried, grilled, cravings so deep it burned. It hurt to want something other than what I had in front of me, other than my life, other than the person next to me.

I stopped for a moment to listen to Sara's jaw as she ate and I couldn't believe how loud it was. That and her slight open mouth chewing made me sick. She was a noisy eater and, the unhappier I became, the more it annoyed me. I'm sure I made her sick, too, in more ways than one, because she often had a grimace on her face when looking my direction.

She overcooked the spaghetti and it was watery with the tomato paste, splashing and slurping with each bite. The sound echoed in the silent room, and I regretted not putting the radio or TV on before sitting down.

'She is as aware of it as I am,' I thought to myself, our eating becoming more mechanical as we try to be quieter. We try to overcome the moment and wait for this tacit realization to pass.

And as if this food isn't inedible enough, the disgust of staring at it as we miserably feed ourselves serves to reinforce our self-pity. Though it does reduce the likelihood of looking up into the room, where we might accidentally exchange glances. Where we might actually give space to seeing one another as human again.

She spoke, and as always her words had the combined goal to cut me down and put everything on my shoulders. Like I didn't know. Like I could do anything to change it at this point. But she chose to be with me. She is still here. She has done nothing to change our or her own situation. So she is in no position to complain. I'm nobody's rescuer or provider, and I was straightforward with her about that. She thought she could change me, or get me to try, but I'm just not that kind of guy.

"The eviction papers came in a week ago with a court date. It's on the refrigerator. I hope you know I'm not going."

'Happy New Year to you too, Sara,' I said to myself. Her tone, not the words, made me lose my waning appetite altogether. Why she didn't tell me about the papers when they came in was beyond me. All I could do was shake my head for a few moments, peering at my plate. I was too tired, too beaten, too depleted to engage. I stopped reacting to her a while back. She wanted only to jab me, at least that's how I saw it, and that's how I felt around her. My verbal retaliation could offer her an opportunity to justify herself as a victim in our predicament. But I wouldn't give that to her. And I could sense her surprise that I had no response. She waited and I felt her eyes move to see me put my fork down, until she gave up and let go of righteously torturing me further. There is nothing to talk about anymore. There is only resentment between us for failing at any kind of real communication.

The only reason she wants to blame me is because she feels helpless and doesn't want to assume responsibility. She never once took initiative to claim her own life, walk away, and do something else. She stays and watches her world fall apart while pointing her finger, expecting I would, could, and should know how to fix this. I never knew what a child she was until now, a scared child with a lot to learn.

It was my apartment originally, shared with a roommate who slept on the couch. I knew him from work, another roofer, and he slept at his girlfriend's place most nights so it worked out good for me. The place was spacious and the rent was reasonable. When I met Sara, she was living at her ex boyfriend's in Queens, and things weren't going well there. A few months later she showed up with a suitcase after a fight between them, and I was happy to share my bed with her. We were in love back then. Everything was different and we were hopeful about our future. After my roommate moved out, she said she could swing half the rent. Things went great for a while, until, well, I don't know. We lost our jobs one by one, spent all we had, and then got so down and out that we couldn't get up again. It created so much frustration between us, frustration that created sourness.

We tried everything, thought of everything, and even considered renting out the living room to someone as a bedroom. We owed everyone money — money they knew they'd never see again when they loaned it to us. If it weren't for the unemployment checks then we wouldn't have food or train money.

If she wants to play the victim, I'm fine with that. If she wants to try to make me out to be the bad guy, I'm fine with that. If she wants to extract more from me, she can try, but there is nothing left. She has no idea the humiliation it has caused me. She thinks I'm stronger than her, or that I should be because I'm the man, but I'm not.

This is who I am, for better or worse. This low point has brought me an awakening of reality and acceptance in its harshest form. I'm jobless, almost homeless, and almost single. Yet all this seems a relief from a life of trying to no avail, only to see the true inadequacy of who I am and what I was born into. I could have tried harder and been smarter. But I had no opportunity that I knew of.

I've been believing that there is something better, someone better, that I should be doing this or that, chasing this or that, saying this or that, buying this or that, needing this or that, desiring this or that, respecting this or that, for my entire life. I'm not sure if it's out of insecurity or unoriginality, or that I've been brainwashed by all the ubiquitous forces in my life. Apart from what I've come to believe, I don't know what is left. I don't know what is pure anymore. I just want to be free.

All my hopes and dreams are pathetic and wasteful fantasies that I've held on to for far too long. They're part of this trauma. Now I just want the basics; a home, a purpose, stability, and a partner. The things most people take for granted. I never wanted anything too fancy before, I just wanted more.

I got up and studied the notice she spoke of, felt my insides drop, then marked the calendar and mindlessly walked over to the couch. I lay on my back, closing my eyes, and sinking into the soft cushions. I wished I were somewhere else. I tried to see a green open field in a far off place, but all I could see was the eviction notice and Sara glaring at me from the table.

It was there, on the letter with a date, certified mail. Yes, this was really happening. I wanted to shut off, but I know there are no pause, fast-forward, rewind, and delete buttons for this existence.

In my mind's eye, I watched myself become nothing. I saw a wrecking ball come down from the sky and crush me through the floor. I saw myself eaten by animals, turning to dust, disappearing like I never existed. I made myself cringe.

Then, in the midst of these thoughts, a dream took over, with euphoric, irrational images. It is sleep redeeming me. Always my dreams are redemption, no matter how random they are. Sleep is the only impunitive escape I know of, and in the worst times in my life it is my only reprieve. It's the only place where none of the worries of this world can bother me. I'm not even sure which side is real anymore, and it doesn't matter.

The next morning, I woke laughing. I couldn't remember the dream but I remembered the feeling of lightness, something so foreign to me now. It was the first full night of rest I had in so long. Worry often had me up as the sun was rising.

I looked around the room. Knowing that my days are numbered here only made me feel more attached to this space. I didn't want to leave this apartment. I'd been here five years and the eviction felt like my home was being stolen out from under me. The way the old wood floors were worn from years of people walking on them, the high ceilings, and the ornate pre-war moldings around the doorways and windows. Even the filthy light switches and rickety cabinets. I felt premature nostalgia seeing how the sweet morning light shone through the windows and traveled across the floor and walls, then over to me, while warming the room. Hearing the squeaky doors, the old windows, the shadows from the window bars, and the way the sun was generous to us in here at all hours. I felt real love for this place in an inexplicable way.

Sara painted the walls sky blue last year when she lost her job. Back then we were using our unemployment checks and free time to make the place better. We thought it would be our only chance between jobs to do so, and did it just in case we started renting it out for extra cash. There was an old black wooden chair in the corner that had a hollow heart at the top and Sara always had her clothes hanging off the back. Her clothes were hanging off everything, as if all furniture were her closet. The drapes were sheer white and the rugs were Oriental style, with lots of reds, golds, and greens. Most everything we found in the trash or bought from a neighborhood stoop sale or thrift shop. Years of collecting here and there, and everything seemed to come together perfectly, like it was all made for us.

The morning dump truck outside was loud, and I could hear the men laughing and throwing the trash in the back of it. I waited as long as I could to open my eyes and commit to the day ahead. When I did, all I could do was stare at the wall and watch the sunlight as it hovered over me like a spirit. Finally, the sun, it is something sacred to feel, if only through windows and only on my bare legs. I could never take the sun for granted, even if I saw it every day. Not after this long, dark winter, and all the ones before that.

It was windy out. I knew this because outside tree branches were moving and sending shadows and light speckles throughout the room. I focused my attention on the window and then the brick building next door. From over its roof I could see the sky; it looked promising. Today felt like a day of possibility. The clouds were few and far between and I missed the brightness it created.

The neighboring building had some apartments that appeared abandoned, but I knew they weren't. People lived in there, for ages, and they had few renovations, if any. Nothing like what had been done to our place. The same slumlord owned the entire block and maybe more, but we never saw him. An elderly Hasidic man, he acquired these properties back when you couldn't give them away. Back when anyone who had anything was running from this area like their life depended on it — which it may have. Crown Heights, Brooklyn. A place I grew to love.

It used to be a poverty- and crime-ridden neighborhood, urban quicksand that consumed all but a few. And there are still remnants of that today. There is a sign around the corner with interchangeable numbers that represent the days since the last shooting. The old Crown Heights is still here, but swiftly shifting into something else.

Wealthy Manhattanites moved here over a century ago and built beautiful homes and brownstones on tree-lined streets. I don't know where they went, but as far as I can tell, the population is split between Jewish and Black areas, and has been for a while now, maybe generations. People like me live here because it's still an affordable part of Brooklyn that's near to the city, or at least it used to be cheap when I first moved here years ago.

Now millennials and hipster transplants are invading, paying top dollar before it's even worth top dollar, driving up the cost of living for the rest of us. Doesn't matter to them if liquor stores, crack houses, dollar stores, and hair and nail salons surround them, they are happy to be in a part of Brooklyn they can afford, jump on the train and get to the parts of the city they want to hang out in.

Locals want to cash in and renovate, sell, rent, Airbnb. Everyone here is doing it for an extra buck if they have a garage, basement, or spare room. And in the span of a few years I've seen the Brooklyn bound subway cars get more and more diverse with different skin colors, classes, and languages.

The only obstacle is getting the last generation out, the ones with rent control and subsidized housing. The ones who pay a fraction of what landlords could fetch, like the people next door. The ones who were raised here, who raise families here, hang out on the stoops with their friends, play cards on sidewalk tables, blast loud music, organize block parties, plant gardens, and shovel snow off the sidewalk after every snowstorm. The ones who deal drugs, have thirty cats in their apartment, the hoarders and the old ladies. Those ones. They never get anything much, not even a paint job, because they don't pay like we do. These are the real Brooklynites, who remember when bodegas didn't sell hummus and soymilk, and when there wasn't a café on every corner. And they're going to get priced out, paid to leave their homes, and shuffled out, which will take all the personality away from this place.

Every year neighborhoods like this die a little bit more. I wonder, where does everyone go after here? How do they start over somewhere else? I liked it how it was when I first moved to this area. When I was the only white guy on the block, when everyone made conversation with me, and when everything was cheaper.

They look at me like I'm no different than any other person gentrifying the area. But I'm older than the newbies, who are kids with cosigners, privilege, and education. I'm different. I don't have options like they do.

Sara was making coffee in the kitchen and I watched her as she sat at the table and waited for it to brew with an old newspaper in her hands, quietly propping myself up on the cushions to get a better view. She looked as bad as I felt. I examined her in detail, because she didn't see me, and I noticed more than I had noticed for a long time, even from this distance. There were so many lines on her forehead and her eyes were sunken in with dark circles; her neck looked bony and her body too; skin dry, sallow, blotchy. It was malnourishment, lack of sleep, too much sleep, lack of sun, stress, the winter elements, same as me. The fear that I unknowingly looked as bad as her crossed my mind and made me feel reluctant to leave the house and be seen in public.

It was age. She probably didn't notice it, or maybe she did. I wouldn't know. It made her look so vulnerable. What do you say when you do begin to see your face lose its youthful grace? Do you go around telling people that you used to be beautiful and hope they see you as you once were? Do you anticipate that people see your wrinkles as clearly as you do and become painfully self-conscious? No, you just go forward with fragile pride, leftover from your young years, deluding yourself in the mirror, knowing you've lost something vital, reassuring yourself that you have time to do it all before you die. I suppose it doesn't really matter. The only pride one can retain is to have so much satisfaction in life that age is nothing to you, because youth isn't anything you need or rely on. Sara doesn't have that luxury and neither do I. In our mid-thirties, we are still deciding what we want to be when we grow up. We can no longer depend on getting chances due to freshness, smiles, and beauty, as we have in the past. And, we are insecure because we have nothing to impress, and nothing to show for our years.

In the same moment that she looked haggard, the sun moved and shone through the window above the kitchen sink. Ah, there, she looked beautiful now. Her fair, delicate skin looked clean. The fatigue on her face looked wise, and her wrinkles looked like old lion scars. I need to stop myself from judging her. I'm sure she has done it to me once or twice, though. I'm sure I've had my moments, moments that lasted weeks, months, or years, where I was a shock to regard as well, in more ways than one.

Looking startled, she turned and saw me watching her. She smiled nervously and blushed, then offered me a cup of coffee. It was too early to hold grudges. I accepted. Guilt. I don't know why I always felt guilty with her. It was partly for ignoring her so often, partly for not being the man that could make her happy or even treat her well, leading her into this mess, lying to her, being shallow and selfish, letting her depend on me when I knew I couldn't feel obligated to her, shutting her out, using her anger as a scapegoat to push her away, and so many other reasons that I did and didn't know. My guilt and confusion was how she bound me to her and she knew it. But, on innocent mornings like this, I felt weak with her, and sometimes I wanted to be.

Coffee continually was a luxury and we were sure never to run out of it, even if we had to steal a few bags, which we always did. With poverty, our morals loosened enough to accept the occasional shoplifting of staple items. Coffee gave us a moment to relax and have the day ahead of us, to be silent together, to feel renewed. My thoughts were so easy in the morning. I could convince myself that I really loved Sara. I could convince myself that today was different and all the loss could be reversed. I could convince myself that I could be the focused person who turns it all around. I could believe that today was a day where change would come upon me effortlessly. I could anticipate my destiny before the day beat me up and threw me to the longest hours ahead, those hours where I wanted to fast forward to the moment I fall asleep and then start over again tomorrow with the same hope as right now.

The coffee was our only real regime and it was a necessity for our well being, like showering. Even if it was decaf, the aroma and the ritual was caffeine itself, was survival, life for the downtrodden in so many ways.

We sat for a bit. She brought over a cup of black coffee with sugar, which she placed on the coffee table, then sat in the chair across from me in silence. Wearing a long hippie dress as a nightgown, she curled up in the back of the big chair and threw a blanket around her shoulders while facing the sunlight, staring blankly out the window, holding the steam to her face from the hot cup. I spoke to her and she turned to look at me. Her clear, red eyes made me uneasy. I told her that I would seriously look for a job starting today, any job. I told her I was sorry and would get us out of this mess and find another situation, whatever it took. And I told her that I loved her and wanted her to be safe. Everything I said came out with true conviction, but I wasn't sure I could make good on my words. It was my morning high talking. I could think about it later and change my fickle mind. I seldom spoke like this, and she was listening intently with her brows furrowed and her forehead scrunched up, because she had been with me long enough to have heard it before. She looked into my eyes, but it wasn't persuading her. It was skeptical encouragement, borne from the bitterness of knowing my game more than I understood it. She didn't want to reveal that my words gave her promise because she didn't want to look stupid for believing them again, but it was what she wanted to hear and there was no denying that. We all need to believe a lie to get through a rough patch, to find a reason to keep things the way we want and need. And I know she'll believe it because she still loves me.

"Listen, baby, look at me. It's gonna happen. I can't promise I'll be able to keep this place, but I can tell you that I'll be working soon and will figure it all out. Please relax and stop being mad at me and give me a chance."

"I hope so, Johny. I really do. We'll see, but I'm not going to hold my breath anymore. I've heard this before."

She might still stay with me if it works out. Or at least I think that's what she meant, that she wanted it to work. She was so afraid to be alone and end up back at her moms. One part of me was hoping to push her away and the other was telling her what she wanted to hear, because I wasn't sure what life would be like without her, or those moments when I needed her. It was a wicked move and I knew it, but maybe she had thoughts to go anyway. Maybe she was no better and no worse than me at this charade. In the end, she might be the one leaving me. She might see me as a stepping-stone that she'll tire of eventually, and walk away leaving me surprised that she actually had the guts to do it.

When we are both destitute and homeless, I don't want to be a gentleman on her account. I don't want to give away what little I have. I can't afford to love her. My miserable state is not one I care to share with her or anyone else. She was right about one thing: we'll see. The fact that I was reading into her reply indicated I was playing games, and my occasional interest in her was only a reaction to her occasional disinterest in me. There was too much and never enough to keep it going.

The apartment was gone to me already, a wash, and I was in suspense for the finale. I had no choice but to wait it out, for the darkness, the cold, the eviction process, in whatever order they all came. I've been down this road before and know how it plays out. But it seemed harder this time, and as shocking as it was familiar. All because I was that much older, wearier, and disgusted with myself.

Sara and I will be like ghosts, wandering around a freezing dark shadow of what was once a home for us. Losing this place was a reflection of our relationship withering away, our optimism about life, our years, waiting for the end in a bond of unhealthy convenience, and desperately holding onto an outdated illusion. She looked like a ghost already and it scared me. Sometimes I think that she might be, and I've been talking to the walls all this time, imagining a relationship when she is just some specter of this house or of my declining mind. Perhaps I went crazy a long time ago, and I can't even accept the ghosts I create for company.

I went to the kitchen and splashed my face with cold water, changed my socks and put my boots on.

"Well, I'm gonna go now. Have a good day," I said awkwardly as I grabbed my coat, looking back at her. She barely looked at me, but half smiled while keeping her stare out the window. I think she wanted me to stay longer and talk with her, keep her company, give her some affection, but I felt strained. The only constant she got from me these days was unavailability.

I left the apartment first so I wouldn't have to walk with her to the subway, in case she wanted to join. We both headed out to 'look for jobs,' a common occurrence of late. It was a job to 'look for jobs.' We departed in the morning and came home after dark, a 10-to-5 of sorts, and who knows what she was doing and who knows what I was doing, but it was probably the same. Perhaps she waited for night like I did, on city benches, roaming with her bones turning to icicles, starving for chance, ideas, charity. Or maybe she was actually looking for jobs but wasting too much time in the process.

Just to have something, just to do something, this is why we endlessly search.

When I got off the train I went straight into Central Park and walked for hours, hoping to tire myself out in every way possible. It started to snow and I still walked. The wind froze my face, fingers, and toes, yet I still walked and waited for the sun when it peeked from the clouds. Sometimes I'd stop and bask in the light, leaning my face towards it, before a cloud came and I'd be on my way again. I was getting used to the numbness of my limbs and walking through it was somehow essential to feeling strong. Strength was the only defense against my feelings of exposure. I was pushing myself, fighting a battle, searching for something, and it's all leading me somewhere. I don't know where and what this is that is leading me, but I need to believe there is a reason.

The sun was free, and it made equals of us all, for the first time in a long time.

I had no idea how to look for a job and I couldn't see how finding one would help my predicament fast enough. Merely it seemed a bandage over a broken leg. No job that I could get would pay enough to live in this city on my own. It would take more than that. It would take a new start, time, consistency, the right connections, and still that's no guarantee. And that's how I put miracles on the plate with finding simple work. It was a way to talk myself out of trying, before I even tried.

    I just don't know if I have what it takes to stick with anything long enough. I just don't know if I can enjoy anything anymore. I don't want to be turned away or ruin a good opportunity. And I just don't know what the right direction is. Nevertheless, I've always been willing to try anything, anyone, and anywhere, that just says 'yes' to me. That's the only route I know of, and I decide later.

    I felt embarrassed to ask for job applications. Not too many work like this anymore; everything is done online as far as hiring and job searching and I don't have a resume or a computer. I don't even have the substance to fill a resume — lack of relevant job history, education, and references. Waiting seemed like the only viable option. Something would come. Something always comes no matter who you are or where you are. Even if it's nothing it is something. Only here, in this city, everything comes faster, but everything leaves faster too, at least for me. All of us are as disposable as the previous and the next.

The sun shone for an hour more and then it went gray as the rain started to come down, lightly at first and then heavy. I ran into a cafe and sat at a table where someone had left their empty cup. Hoping to pass as a customer, I held it. I tried to read a newspaper and relax, but I couldn't concentrate and instead became distracted by a few heads that turned to eye me. And it's no wonder they did. I must look like a bum, with my five-day-old beard growing in, my greasy, shaggy wet hair, the hobo combination of an undersized coat with sleeves that didn't near reach my wrists, and an oversized pair of jeans with rips. I had lost ten pounds and all my clothes were baggy. The only thing that still fits are my sneakers, and they are ragged.

I had a fear of looking indigent, which is how I felt people were seeing me. I was ashamed to appear poor and sloppy, because that wasn't me. That isn't who I am. I had been a hard worker in my life and I didn't want to be reduced to that in a glance because of my clothes. But who is anyone to judge, and who am I to care? I had no image to speak of anyhow.

I ran out into the rain using the newspaper as a makeshift hat until it turned into a soggy flop of gray matter with ink covering my palms. I found a church to hide in for a while. A few others were waiting it out, and they huddled at the edge of cover on the stairs. Three women stood near the holy water and one smiled at me. I dipped my finger in the water and walked past, quickly looking down and smiling. They seemed the type to make some kind of chitchat, maybe about god, maybe to be friendly, maybe to see if they could awaken my Christianity now that I've stepped back into a church. I wasn't in the mood and didn't have anything to say. My purpose here is utilitarian, but I can perform the rituals and be respectful.

There were only four others in the pews ahead of where I

sat. All of them looked as though they had come here for worship. They were kneeling and had these plastic bonnets on their head, like rain gypsies. I got on my knees, too.

All I could think of was going to church as a kid, a Catholic church much like this one, with my parents. In the pew — standing, kneeling, sitting, standing, kneeling, singing — and falling asleep to the monotonous tone of the priest's voice. Staring at the frescoes, statues, and stained glass windows portraying angels and devils, the light shining through made me feel like I was in an old world.

There was a statue of Mary near where my mother and I would always sit, and she was stepping on a snake with her hands in prayer and her eyes rolled up. Religion was all so strange to me — the stories, the people, and the rigidity. The women from the holy water walked past and looked at me again. I was afraid that in my lost state I could fall prey to anything that could console me, or anyone who spoke kindly to me. I avoided eye contact and kept my head down.

My parents went through the motions of churchgoing because that's what was expected of them, because they believed in the stories word for word. They tried to be a normal family for a short while, at least for show.

After my dad left, my mother continued bringing me to church, and I increasingly grew to dislike it. There were too many rules, similar to school, but worse. Sitting here I thought of my old man. He liked when I called him 'pops,' and for the first time in a while I let myself think of him. He would hold my hand while we sat in the pew, and shoot me a smile and a silly face now and again. I hadn't seen him in over 25 years, and he's an old man now, though I don't know his exact age. I wonder if he has ever tried to see me, or if he thinks of me, or if he remarried and had more children, or if he's in a coffin somewhere and nobody could find me to tell me he died. Maybe my mom knows and said nothing. She never talked about him after he left. He was erased from our lives and I was better off for it.

Pops. He was a typical drunk, truck driver by day, belligerent piece of shit by night. I'll never forget the scowl on his face each day as he entered the house with his already half-emptied flask, miserable just to look at my mother and me, miserable that another day of his life was spent in the trap of family life, commitment, and responsibility. I think if I had got married and had a child in that horrid setting, I might have been half as surly as him, though that didn't soften my hatred of him one single bit. Despite remembering him in these recollections, I could not remember his face in detail or imagine what he would look like now. His eyes could have been blue or brown and I wouldn't know. I wouldn't know if I saw him in front of me or heard him speak. All I remember is that he was jolly looking with a red face and curly reddish brown hair like a leprechaun. Everybody thought he was a 'good guy' and asked about him, and he was always one to joke with people. Nobody that knew him would ever suspect this man could abuse and desert his family. They would never see what he was capable of, the hurt he caused my mother and me, and how he left us with nothing. He was such a selfish man, and could never comprehend the damage he caused. In his mind he was just doing what he had to do and damn anyone who expected anything out of him. Nothing was his fault. I'm positive his side of the story made my mother and me look like villains who forced him out. But he wasn't someone that would ever explain himself to anyone or talk much of his personal life, so he probably said nothing of us to anyone, ever.

There were no apologies the next day when he stumbled home at 2 a.m., knocking everything over and waking us up by dragging us out of bed. In fact, he would be even more defensive if we brought it up. Mom was ashamed by what he put her through. I remember one night he terrorized us until the early hours, chasing her as she tried to fight back and keep him away from hurting me, too, until he hit her so hard she was knocked unconscious. I went back to my room and cried all night thinking she had died, and he never came in to check up on me. She couldn't look at either of us for days, and he never once acted repentant but pushed us away even more. All he did was get quiet, avoid us, and cut down his drinking for a few days. He disappeared just a few calm weeks after that and mom and I never spoke of it or him again. He stole many of the valuable items from the house when he left — the jewelry, television, and even some of my prized baseball cards. I don't know if it was out of spite, need, or a desire to completely ruin everything in his wake for all of our sakes. He knew he was losing control and couldn't stop.

    The abuse became a habit, an addiction, and his fear shut him down to facing us. I believe he left because he knew he'd never be able to live it down or change, and he was afraid he'd wake up from a blackout and see he did something he couldn't walk away from, and for which he couldn't forgive himself. It stained us with sadness, like we caught his sickness.

    I hated remembering that night. It's one of those vivid memories that sink my stomach every time it involuntarily flashes into my mind. There were many nights like that, but none so detrimental. None of us could look at each other the same way after that. Many times that memory made me want to find him and kill him, or at least hurt him. I wanted to shove my anger in his face and destroy him, like he destroyed us, like he destroyed my chances for a regular childhood, for a regular life.

    After dad left, mom worked doubles all night or all day to keep up with rent and bills. She wanted me to go to church by myself, saying it was good for my soul. But she knew I never went unless she was with me, and I think in a way she was glad when I stayed home. She didn't want to leave me alone so often, but times were tough. Nobody helped her out. There was no family on her side. They were either dead or disgraced by her life choices, and believed it was her fault that my dad left. She didn't tell them all the horrible details, but they had an idea, and probably still would have blamed it on her for not being able to control him. None of them were really that nice, anyway. Just harsh, old fashioned religious types who talked about each other constantly, and looked down on those that were worse off than them.

The only time I ever felt like a success was when I compared myself to dad. I spoke to myself, 'At least I'm not a drunk, you scumbag.'

My parents both passed their dysfunction onto me, and it was the only thing that linked us — a bond, a curse, a black cloud that would never let us go. That was the only feeling I had when thinking of them. And as much love as I felt for my mother, I just kept losing contact with her.

I found myself praying with all my might. I knelt and clasped my wet hands together while the words repeated in my head, 'Please God, help me, please help me.' Whatever it meant, whatever it could bring, anything at all.

The kind of atheist prayers that come out in last resort panic, the kind meant for God or the devil, whoever comes first. I speak them to God but the devil is also on my mind. God is too slow, and technology has replaced him anyway. I'm not sure anyone is listening here except some lost angels in this church.

I tried to focus on what I could do with the rest of the day, but it didn't take long for me to get distracted. I found myself looking at the floor wondering if the rain had stopped. The rain brought out the smell of the marble and dusty scents of the church. There was still an echo of a downpour, but I wasn't sure if my ears were playing tricks on me. It didn't matter. I had nowhere to be. I had nowhere to run. I could hide out here for as long as I needed.

I refuse to be a broken-downer, as my dad used to say, aka a 'bum'. I'd seen those people wandering around, their skin torched by the elements. They get no mercy, nobody wants them, they go insane, they drink, they drug, and they get stepped over. They rest in train platforms and train cars, parks, and other public establishments. People only want to sweep them under a rug because nobody speaks for them, because they don't exist; they are lazy, crazy, irrelevant, addicted, and resource-less. They made their life like this and deserve what they get, out of sight and out of mind. The general population wants to be rid of these people. And we are able to look down on them indifferently with our noses up because we have some stroke of luck not to turn out like them. The worst kind of profiling exists for these outcasts, and nobody cares because they are weak. Nobody cares because it doesn't affect them. There was and never will be a rally for the 'bums.' They wouldn't even be there to fight for themselves. They are invisible. They are dangerous. They are laughable and they are sad, but somehow they make us feel better about ourselves. People are always stepping on those that they can, and someone else is doing the same to them.

Everything is so relative; you can open your eyes to one thing, but still be blind to another. I never noticed these people before, but the closer I got to their state, the closer I looked at them, and the more I thought about them. They live in this gray area of life. I didn't really understand or know what to think of them, but I'll have a better idea soon.

Outside the rain was such a light sprinkle that the streets started to crowd with people again, flooding out from under awnings, cafes, and lobbies. Everyone rushing. Anyone who's anyone has somewhere to be, someone to see, something to do, something to sell, something to make. Some are waiting just to go, just to get, just to feel, just to fill, a little more into an empty place. None of us even know why we do the things we do. We're on puppet strings.

It's just how fast everything moves and how fast you expect it to move. It's just who you're comparing yourself and others to. It's just who you're listening to. It's just the impatience and fear you feel of constantly wanting more, because you're exposed to this idea of having and being more, getting this and that and then the next. I don't know that if I had more I'd be any happier. I've seen the proud and the lavish and even they can't stand to face themselves. There is equality here: our collective discontent and insecurity, and it's well disguised by those with the most to hide. The rich wander as much as the poor, and everyone in between. Busy doing nothing, and everything, just to drive and survive. Just to be blind.

And there is no place else to be.

In the streets I watch people pass me. Their faces are so sharp after the rain. Nobody looks perfect. The light reveals us. I feel so isolated that everyone looks and seems exactly the same.

For two hours I walked into every quasi-appropriate establishment that I could. I talked to a few managers. I lied about job experience among other things. There was always a different story that rolled off my tongue. But I think many of these people were humoring me, just pretending to give me a fair shot. I saw their eyes scan me in contemplation, though I didn't care if when I left they spoke badly of me. I'd need some new clothes to take this job hunt seriously, perhaps a shave and shower. And, most importantly, I'd need to grow some teeth.

Later that evening I walked in to find Sara sitting at the table. Suddenly she was scrambling to make like she was busy, grabbing a pen in her hand and starting to write something. She was probably staring at the wall and debating making more coffee, waiting for me to finally come home.

I went over to her and kissed her head. I didn't want to be distant from her, but sometimes she drove me crazy. It was a consolation that we both acted like over-dramatic nuts, but had each other when we needed to laugh about it. Tonight, however, I was relieved to see her face. I felt adrift, just like her, and she was my security blanket.

"I managed to get $100 from my uncle," she said, looking up at me, reaching into her pocket and dropping a bunch of mixed bills on the table.

"Oh yeah, baby, let's go get some real food! I'm starving!"

I kissed her on each cheek a few more times and laughed. She looked taken aback by my attention, happy that she found a way to please me and pull me back in. We were like little kids that had money for the ice cream truck. I wanted to kiss her again on the lips but I couldn't, and she saw that I refrained. It meant so much more to her than it did to me, and it wasn't fair. It always made me pity her that she could settle for so little for herself and so little from me. She loves to delude herself. But, if it's enough for her, it's enough for me.

Tonight we would eat well. Tonight we would forget for a moment and walk through the icy air, laughing and holding hands like best friends, to buy as much junk food as we could eat for today and tomorrow. Tonight she would try to touch me, but I would find some excuse to refuse, and she would know deep down that it was a lie.

*****

A few weeks later things were finally looking up. I signed a paper in court with the landlord's lawyer, agreeing to have the rest of January and all of February to move. He seemed sympathetic to our circumstance, but I think he wanted to avoid more court appearances. Dragging it out would just cost them time and money. After that we would have to get out or else a sheriff would lock the doors, so the lawyer said. It wasn't bad, and although I could have prolonged it, taken it to trial, and maybe got an extra month or two, I just wanted to be done with it. The weight of it was too much, and signing the paper gave me an end date that I could to work with.

    Sara found a job. An uppity café in Prospect Heights, intellectuals, overpriced bitter coffee, fancy sandwiches, scones, and macaroons, that sort of stuff. She had the retro look by default, with messy hair and mismatched vintage clothes, and fit right in with the look of the other workers. The pay was just five dollars above minimum wage, which hardly covered our necessities. It didn't change our situation but we were a step up from before. I got to save the few hundred dollars I had left from my last unemployment check, of which I kept to myself. There was no point in paying any of the bills; we were in too deep for that.

    Sara said tips were pretty good. She said it was different every day, but she did better in that department than from her hourly rate. My cell bill was taken care of and I had a phone number to follow up on my job prospects, which were few and unambitious. The refrigerator was full of leftovers from the café and some food she managed to sneak home — tomatoes, cheese, avocados, bread, and leftover muffins. We didn't have to buy food or coffee at all anymore. It didn't hurt my pride to take her money every day for various expenses. I could continue living off her for as long as needed. If anything, it gave me a boost of confidence to have something in my pocket and not have to feel like I was on the brink anymore.

At the table she sat reading a magazine, probably taken from the café, while I sat on the couch going through job posts on my phone. She started looking up at me, and I saw her take her tip pouch out of her bag and empty all the bills and change on the table, proceeding to count. I had a feeling she had something to say, and I tried to look occupied.

I knew it was something I didn't want to hear. Those 'talks' always come out of the blue like that and have so much premeditation behind them that you have no response, because it's usually the truth. I knew it was coming, eventually. We hadn't fought for a while and were amicable, but there were still so many unanswered questions, on her part, that I knew she held onto. She brought issues up before and nothing was ever resolved then. I'd always deny and diffuse everything, and she'd always come back and go on a little longer. I was hoping that she'd let them go, but also that things could go on unchanged. The only answer for her questions meant admitting that I am not in love nor am I attracted to her anymore, and I couldn't say that.

"So anyway, what are your plans when we have to leave this place? Seeing as though we won't really be able to afford a place on my income alone."

I understood that with her new money she had been thinking of some better independent options. She'd been working a short time, but it was enough for her to feel like she could do better. Though she said it while counting coins, looking cool as can be, like we were just roommates figuring out who was going to move out first.

I replied, "Well, I don't know. I was thinking I could finally nail down a job, and we'll swing a month-to-month room or something in a cheap area."

I ignored all that I understood her to say. It had been so long since I kissed her, made love to her, or treated her with care, and here I was acting like we were partners. Here I was acting like I wanted to be with her when a few weeks ago I was ready to shake her at the first sign of difficulty. I gave nothing to the relationship and she had finally, and suddenly, outgrown me. Out of the corner of my eye, I could see her scowling.

"I got some good leads at the moment. Expecting a call back any day now. Don't worry sweetie, I got us covered."

As I spoke I sunk back into the sofa cushions, peering out the east facing windows and reaching for my cell phone to nervously fiddle with. I looked up to find her with her face down, shaking her head from side to side as if to say, 'no more.' It was the look of a woman who has had enough. I'd seen it many times before, and I was afraid. She threw the money down on the table, stood up, walked over to the kitchen counter and leaned against it, facing me. Here she was with cash and power on her side of the field, for a change. But, more than that, she was starting to trust her intuition.

"Okay, Sara, come right out and say it: You hate me. You've got this great life now serving coffee and lavender muffins and all of a sudden I'm the biggest loser in the world. I mean, I carried your weight for a year in this place! Not only that —"

"AHA!" She screamed.

"You carried me? That's bullshit and you know it. I was getting unemployment checks, too, and paying the bills and half the rent. You're an asshole, and I'm glad to finally be opening my eyes to it! UGH! You've been using me for so long! You won't even look into my eyes or touch me. It's all so phony and I can see right through it. I don't know why it took me so long. How can you live with yourself? No wonder you hate yourself so much!"

I can't say her words didn't hurt, or that I didn't feel she was right. I knew that it was only a matter of time until she would discover this, especially now that she had this job and a few friendly coworkers to confide in. My only surprise was that it happened so abruptly and that she had been so angry with me, which I deserved. Her words left me in pieces, and although she has said worse to me, this time I knew we wouldn't be making up. Knowing the truth, she couldn't forgive this seeming deception on my part. I had selective memory for what others did for me or how my words and actions affect others. I know. What a crumb I am. I went as far as I could and truly didn't mean to hurt her, but now I see that I really did. She cared for me. I didn't have the guts to turn down easy company, or have the guts to walk away when I knew I didn't love her like I used to. I didn't even have the guts to let her go, be alone, and be honest. I'm an opportunist. It wasn't that I used her; it was that I wanted her to settle for the minimum from me.

"Sure, then the real question, or the real answer, is that this is over. I've been trying with you, but you push me away, and I don't need to be taken care of or be accused of using you just because you're not getting what you want. I'm not going to defend this nonsense when I've done nothing wrong, or put up with this angry lashing. I never asked you to give me anything, or expected anything from you. Please, Sara, go do what you want, be with who you want, I don't care. I need a break. You can stay here until the doors lock as far as I'm concerned. I knew this would happen, and all I can say is great, good for you. Really, good for you. Bravo. I'm glad you're moving up in the world with your latte buddies."

And, having said that, I got up, grabbing the coat off the back of the chair and walking out the door, hoping I'd never have to go back there and see her face. Hoping she'd feel bad for hurting me, hoping she'd feel sorry, believe my deflections, and also hoping she'd wait out the time and continue to bring me food and give me money. When I last saw her face after speaking she looked blank, almost as though she was shocked that after all these years that was all she got out of me. But this time she was hoping for something more, believing deep down maybe I loved her in my own fucked up way, which I did. Maybe she was looking for a heartfelt response where I admit my fears and earn her mercy while begging her to stay. Maybe she was looking for a hint of care and emotion, so she could muster an excuse to hold onto me, forever hold onto me, but finally realized there was none and never will be. Maybe she was hoping I would get on my knees and cry like a baby. But all she got was me walking away, because that's what I wanted.

I know she saw how much time and energy she wasted on being with me. It was a waste of time for both of us. We did each other no favors.

Yes, Sara, you have wasted years on me and you feel unlovable. It's the same way I have felt with others who broke my heart, and now I'm doing it to you. I am a bad person. Thank god we never got married and had kids or I'd be like my father.

I wish I could say it were true, that I didn't love her, but I couldn't. But she wouldn't see it that way, because from her end it felt like I didn't, when it was just a lack of desire. I deeply loved her, in an attached sort of way. I have insulted this woman rather than just being upfront with her. She might have eventually understood, and we could have been friends down the road. I had no gauge of love because I never had any success with it. I didn't know if love was time, comfort, trust, forgiveness, attraction, passion, or infatuation. They pulled forward, and I pulled back. I pulled forward, and they pulled back. I wasn't giving them something, or they weren't giving me something. That was all. I found ways to stay clamped up by choosing other clamped up people. But what was I supposed to say? What does someone say in that situation? I can't make any more promises, nor can I lie about this one thing: it is over. I have nothing to give to it. And for some reason unknown to me, I never valued her.

After an hour walking the streets of Brooklyn, I took the train into the city and roamed up to Central Park and beyond as the sky turned black and blue. It felt like a Sunday but I had no idea if it was.

There was an initial relief to clearing the slate and starting fresh. It was a buzz, and a welcome ending of this chapter. The fear of starting over would soon set in, the fear of being alone, moving on to do things I have no clue how to do, which are difficult and require work. I'd been through these break-ups too many times before. The problem being that I find myself falling into the same sort of cycle again, and the same patterns unconsciously follow me.

Needing a distraction from myself throws me back into the cycle, because I have no idea how to go any other direction. It's like I have no control over it, like I'm programmed by some deficiency to repeat the same mistakes in every relationship. I've been so close a few times to real change, but relapsed and perpetuated the absurdity that seems to come naturally to me. Progress has come so slowly in my life and has been reversed as quickly as a change in mood. Perhaps I love torturing myself, and find different ways to keep others and myself on an edge.

At this point I would rather sleep in Central park. I'm mortified to see her after dragging her this far. The night air was freezing yet my nerve kept me going. 'We'll see, Sara,' I said to myself. Only time would tell. Only time could tell. I had nothing to lose but time, yet I had so much of it.

In the park between two big boulders, I found a narrow space and lay in it, looking up at the stars and keeping my hands up my sleeves for warmth. With my hat pulled down almost over my eyes, my hoodie zipped up and covering half my face, I still felt cool drafts seeping through every opening they could find. This frosty air was as penetrable as water. The skyline was visible and the lights sparkled in the cold against a dark palette. There was so much going on in my mind that I felt I might never sleep. I wanted to die, and yet I was curious about life beyond this phase, life beyond this relationship that I've felt stuck in for so long.

Whatever high I had earlier was wearing off and replaced with anguish so deep that I cried. Things could always get worse, that's one truth I've learned in life. My coping skills were getting stronger with age, but sensitivity was taking over and I welcomed and rejected it. The thought of losing Sara was harder than I thought it would be. The thought of losing the apartment was harder than I thought it would be. The thought of losing my belongings was harder than I thought it would be. It was all going to happen, and was beyond my control. Especially because I was seeing it all could have been avoided with minimal effort to get out there and try anything, anything at all.

I've tried so hard, in thought, but haven't gotten anywhere of true substance. I've had so much stress and pressure, in thought, and haven't achieved anything. I don't know anymore what would have been harder; to do what I wanted to do or to only think of doing it.

The air ripped through me all the more as my will was breaking down. For a long hour I fell in and out of sleep and awoke to such harshness in my heart. 'Enough of this,' I thought. I am not homeless yet. There is still a warm home to return to. She is still there to feel safe near. Everything is still there. Under the cozy blankets, her warm body could be next to me. I had no idea how anyone could do this, how anyone could be homeless. It was consuming right to the core. It was enough to freeze to death.

In the morning I woke to the sound of Sara getting ready for work and making coffee. Every movement she made seemed to slam — the doors, the cups, the cabinets, the drawers, the coffee machine. She wasn't trying to be quiet to prevent me from waking. I'm sure it was on purpose.

She was still furious. She was still holding on, expecting change. I got home at 2 a.m. and slept on the couch, even though I wanted to be in the bed with her. I watched her sleep, studied her face over and over and almost woke her to tell her that I felt so alone and needed her. But I wanted to let her stop loving me, and be mad so that she could walk away and find someone worthy. More than that, I was unable to show her such vulnerability in myself. I imagine she waited for me to come home and say something like that. We were both so proud and stubborn and would continue this relentless cold war until the very end. And, I knew that I finally needed to walk away from this, too.

When she left for work, I was able to get up and walk around the apartment in peace. I went to take a shower only to find the water was cold, gas finally shut off. No wonder she was banging everything this morning. I checked the kitchen clock and it was still ticking away. The electricity was still on. The waiting game had officially begun.

I bravely washed my hair in the cold kitchen sink water, grabbed some decent-looking clothes from the bottom of my drawer, the last of the clean laundry, and then shaved with warm water that I boiled in the electric kettle.

The place wasn't so cold, which was probably because we were on the third floor and got a lot of heat from below. But the cold water was brutal. It would be tougher for Sara since she loved hot showers and sometimes took two in one day, just standing there under the steamy water. We could never take showers together because she would always make it hotter and hotter, and I'd get scorched while she laughed at me.

We'd find a way to take showers, even if it meant getting a membership at a cheap fitness club that had a promotion. I already knew of a place I could go and I'm sure she did too.

Looking in the mirror, all cleaned up, I saw that I still had it. I still had a handsome face with chiseled features. My skin looked good despite it being pale. I hadn't looked at myself in the mirror for a long time, and my face seemed different to me now that it was shaven. Perhaps I had gained some weight and it filled me out more. It always puzzled me, coming from two unattractive parents, that I ended up with good looks. It was part of the reason I never went single for too long, part of the reason I had an ego, part of the reason I got too many second chances in life and blew them all knowing there'd be more. Part of the reason Sara stuck around, like the women before her. Today I would try to use my looks to get ahead in the nicer parts of town; no more labor jobs that get me nowhere and leave me with a broken back. Appealing to the superficiality of looks was something reliable, but it had an expiration date, and I needed to get my ass moving.

On the train I looked at pretty girls and they almost always looked back. It was all I needed for a boost, no matter how silly it was. I needed it and it gave me energy. All I needed to know was that they were returning my gaze. All I needed to know was that I was still desirable.

"Are you hiring by chance?"
"No, but you can fill out an application."
"Are you hiring by chance?"
"I'm not sure, but the manager will be back in an hour and you can come back then and ask."
"Would you be hiring by any chance?"

"You would have to go to our website and fill out an application or submit a resume online via the employment opportunities tab."
"Are you guys hiring?"
"Come back tomorrow and talk to Gus.
"Are you hiring?"
"No."

It gets harder and harder to get rejected, but easier to lower my expectations.

I walked past a dog grooming salon and it looked like something I could do, and like. 'Uptown Dogs' read the sign. There was a golden retriever inside and, when he saw me, his tail started wagging. Something pulled me in. I had no experience with dogs as far as grooming and care, but it seemed a no-brainer.

When I walked in I saw two Asian men in their late forties to early fifties, sitting in chairs facing each other and laughing at something one of them had just said. They were dressed meticulously in designer clothes and had a very polished look. One of them was much more conservative in appearance than the other, his hair slicked back, donning preppy, black fitted clothing, loafers, and delicately gold-rimmed glasses. The other looked like an upscale hipster with his hair purposefully disheveled, wearing a fuchsia vintage blazer and pale blue pants.

In the back was a window overlooking twenty plus dogs in a large room, all barking and playing. All of them were pristine, the dogs of the Upper West Side, as the sign stated, and most likely pure breeds. Through another window, a small dog had just been washed and was getting blown dry by a kid, probably in his early twenties. Both men looked at me and then looked at each other, deciding who would speak first, seeming to question what someone like me wanted stumbling into a place like that. I was more nervous in their presence than at all the other places I'd entered, and as funny as it felt to be standing there with their eyes on me, and the noise of the dogs in the background, I spoke without hesitation and asked if they needed any help.

Again they looked at one another as if to decide who would reply, and the conservative one with the glasses took the reins.

"Well, yes, we might be looking for someone."

He said it carefully, just in case he had to take it back. I nodded.

"Why don't you have a seat and I'll ask you a few questions right now. Do you have some time?"

"Yes, yes, I do. Right now is good," I replied, taking a chair and attempting to speak and sit professionally.

The other one offered me coffee or tea, and I accepted. I never turn down a cup of coffee. Black with two sugars. All the while we talked over the loud barking from just beyond the door; it was hard to get used to. I missed a few words here and there, but was getting enough to understand. The golden retriever, the only dog loose in front, sat by my chair and I started petting him as I spoke, which they seemed to like. The big dog would look up at me occasionally and wince, with his large, pink tongue hanging out the side of his mouth.

I saw from first glance that they were a gay couple. They looked fancy, but not too far from down-to-earth underneath their slick exteriors. Overall I got a good feeling about them. They were relaxed, and you know when you encounter those types because you're at ease to be yourself. I liked that I got to interview with them on the spot, minus all the hoops other places wanted me to jump through, with resumes, appointments, callbacks, and so forth.

The three of us sat talking for nearly 40 minutes. They asked questions about my past jobs, where I live, how long

I've been in the city, and where I'm from originally. I made up mostly everything I told them, but I didn't feel as though I was lying, just rearranging facts to make myself sound better. The stories were borrowed and exaggerated, with a healthy dose of point blank white lies, and some honesty — or at least my version of it. I hoped I could remember these stories later, if I got the job.

All the useful information I recounted was recycled. They asked me if I ever had a dog. I said 'yes' and described my former neighbor's dog to a tee, a small, hyper rescue mutt who was always jumping on Sara and me, and would choke herself on the leash every time she was walked. Raja was her name. She belonged to two hippies that lived across the hall from us for a few months last year, maybe more. Somehow they ended up in our neighborhood but disappeared pretty fast. They were the sort that had tapestries all over their walls and incense burning. That kind. Jeremiah and Cat. They moved out before the winter hit, to live in a bus and drive around the country with Raja. We hadn't heard from them since and knew we wouldn't, but they promised a postcard. I'm sure they are living somewhere beautiful, somewhere I'd rather be.

Sara and I were close to them for a while, and remember when they first brought Raja home from the shelter. It was fun playing with her, and she was so sweet that we debated getting a dog of our own. We secretly thought it might bring our relationship back. But, when I lost my job at the moving company, we decided not to add to our responsibilities. The story has now changed to Raja being our dog, Sara's and mine, and Sara taking the dog after our breakup then moving out to California. And it seemed to go over well with them because they collectively let out an, "Oh, how sad."

I was amused that they must have thought I named my dog Raja, if they noticed, but I couldn't think of another name. Then again, they probably assumed my girlfriend named her, the kind of girl that takes off to California with a dog.

When I told them I lived in Crown Heights that was all they wanted to talk about. They told me stories of how they lived there when they first moved to NYC, before Brooklyn was hip.

The one who offered me the coffee walked over and put his hand on his partner's shoulder as he was laughing and telling stories of what craziness and charm they remembered there. He asked me which streets I lived off of and I told him, but he didn't seem to know where it was. I bet they lived on the border to prospect heights, a much nicer area than I lived in, because I just couldn't picture them in my hood, not ever. Back when they claimed to live there it was a real dangerous ghetto.

I had started filling out an application, but people came in to pick up their dogs so they told me not to bother with the rest, just my name, address, and phone number would do. All good signs. When I walked out the door I felt confidant. And I managed to stop by a few more businesses while I was feeling good, restaurants and café's, clothing stores, filling out more applications before heading home.

Lee was the name of the conservative one with the glasses, and Chris was the cool looking one in the blazer. They got up when I left, which I appreciated, and I told them I hoped to hear from them soon, to which they smiled.

I had a hunch that I'd hear from Chris and Lee again. I could see myself there more than I saw myself working anywhere else.

*****

Almost a month later, there I was walking and grooming dogs, working alongside Lee and Chris every day. I liked it even more than I thought I would. Sara was gone, for almost three weeks now. One day she had packed a few bags and left while I was at work. When I got home I knew right away. It was the only thing that finally made me respect her, even though it meant losing her. I'd anticipated it and it was more painless than I imagined. There was no conversation after the last fight, not a peep. I was neither surprised nor did I miss her as much as I thought I would. I wished her well in my mind and meant it, or tried to. It was a release, truly, but I think if I hadn't been working I would have taken it much harder.

The only problem, the biggest problem still, was that I was soon to be homeless. I tried to avoid thinking of it, but here it was in front of me, and quickly approaching. I didn't make enough money to transfer to another apartment, if there was even one in my budget. Not to mention, I had bad credit, terrible job history, lack of long-term employment, and lack of references. In other words, I would never get approved for any kind of lease agreement, cash in hand or not. New York operates more formally than it used to, and more formally than other areas. Every place wants an income and credit check, tax returns, to see your substance in numbers, and I've worked under the table for too long. Every roommate situation available seemed to be with twenty year olds, and they didn't want me either. I'm an old man in their eyes. I really didn't want to live with anyone else, especially people I had nothing in common with. If something is affordable and isn't asking for a whole bunch of paperwork, it surely is a dump, and in a bad neighborhood way out on the outskirts of the boroughs.

I continued with my life and didn't tell Lee and Chris anything about the eviction. They would scrutinize me for it or, even worse, try to help me, which would only make me uncomfortable. I didn't deserve help and I couldn't accept it.

Already I felt indebted to them and they knew it. I was eager to please and help out, never saying no, always trying to do more than was expected. They were happy to unload most of the workload on me and, although I'm sure they liked it, I'm also sure if I hadn't done any of it they would have liked me just as much. This job saved my life. All I ever did before was manual labor jobs, and that was just the way it was. But this job was sweet, easy, fun, and I was making a good wage. I enjoyed it so much that I didn't even feel like I was working. And they trusted me. They hadn't given me a key yet, but they talked about that coming real soon.

Lee and Chris loved dogs. Without a doubt this place was their passion. They treated every dog that was dropped off like a child, greeting them with a hug, an ear tweak, and a big smile. I was almost convinced that they liked dogs more than people, and I didn't blame them. I seemed to be leaning towards that feeling, too. It was great to see every one of them walking in with their tails wagging.

But what Chris and Lee really loved most seemed to be their socialite scene. I'd never been in proximity to this world, and it was glamorous and exciting to me, if not enviable. There were always friends stopping by, lunch dates and dinner parties, shows, concerts, and upstate weekend retreats. They were always on the phone planning the next event, and they always knew what was happening in the city on what night and who was going to be there. Seeing how social they were made me realize what a lone wolf I had always been. I never really explored this city. I can't say if it was a lack of money, friends, ideas, or all of the above. I just never thought of it.

If I had to choose between them, which one I liked more, I'd choose Chris. He was nicer, whereas Lee treated me like a lap dog, sending me off to run personal errands for him — dry cleaning, latte fetching, and so on. I didn't mind it, but I liked that Chris wasn't the kind to treat me like a personal servant. He was normal, free of hang-ups. Lee just acted like a fool most the time and always had something up his sleeve.

Chris was also the one who taught me the most about the dogs. He took the time to teach me about handling and training, and he really knew his stuff. Lee never had much input, none that he shared with me anyway. It seemed to me that the love for the place came from Chris and the network and organizing came from Lee. They made a good couple for it, and they had a booming business. Location was perfect. They even sold high-end dog foods and pet products, which brought in a lot of money. Lee was always talking and drumming up sales. People were throwing them money without hesitation, anything for the dogs. And I mean anything.

Hopefully this job won't be one where things go wrong. Not this one. I liked them too much and I liked helping with the dogs. I just never know how things will end up. I've had so many jobs in the past that went awry all of a sudden, and bridges were burned. As long as they treated me good there would be no reason for that to happen, but I couldn't know that, and I couldn't know that it wouldn't be my fault.

Every day I showed up at 9 a.m. sharp. Lee and Chris were already there, sorting who was in doggie daycare, grooming, and training. There was a lot more to it than I would have expected. Most of the dogs were in general pop in this one big playroom. They were always playing and trying to hump each other and it was funny to watch. They were like little kids but easier.

The dogs started to make me happier each day. I found myself looking forward to their arrival. Their different faces and personalities were growing on me. On our walks, I tried to spread my love evenly amongst them. There was an art to it, and I was developing my own style. Chris said that I was a natural, and that he'd teach me how to train them soon.

Every day I took them out in groups of three for 30 minutes, and that lasted until all that needed a walk were walked. It almost took all day when we had a full house and Chris and Lee would handle the grooming and training themselves. One dog drew me in the most: Bella. A rescue that this young couple adopted somewhere during their travels in Asia. She had the look of a scrappy street puppy. She was light brown with yellowish eyes, a medium sized dog, with a tail that curled up like a husky. Once she started to trust me, she completely came out of her shell. That dog chose me. Chris and Lee said Bella was never interested in anyone before I came around.

While we walked, her eyes watched me move so that she could keep close to my side and follow my movements. When I hesitated, she hesitated. When I stopped, she stopped. When I quickened my pace, she quickened her pace. When we sat she would sit by my side and look up at me. I always saved her for the last walk, which was hard because I waited all day while she gave me sad eyes. I'd take two other small dogs with her on the walk so that I could manage it all easier for her benefit. In the park we always went to the same place on top of a rock by the reservoir. I held the smaller dogs on one side, and Bella on the other. It was in those moments that I felt some solace. Bella always snuck licks on my face, and as I started laughing she would get her tongue in my mouth. I didn't mind one bit. I wished I could take her home, just for one night. If she were sitting on my couch with me, sleeping on my bed, watching a movie, I would be happy, and I wouldn't feel so alone. I wouldn't feel like I needed anyone but her.

There was nobody that I had a connection to anymore, no real friends to speak of, no family besides a mother whom I sparsely contact, no social life, no colleagues, just a succession of failed relationships and neglected friendships. My voice constantly echoed in my own head and I became so accustomed to it that I couldn't imagine it any other way. I was so deep in my own world that sometimes when I'd hear someone's voice, I'd jump. In spite of it all — the confusion, the question of any future stability — my time with Bella made me forget it all. She was the goofiest, cutest thing I'd ever seen, and my only regret was that I didn't get a dog years and years ago. It might have saved me from some rough times.

The only obstacle at work was dealing with Lee's condescending attitude towards me. It became more and more of a challenge and he got more and more brazen with his entitled behavior, constantly seeing how much more I would take. When I'd had enough of him for the day, he sensed it, and would then get really nice all of a sudden. I didn't see how Chris tolerated it. They were so different. Chris could have done better, but maybe Lee had the money. I couldn't see any other reason why Chris would put up with him. Apart from them both being Asian and gay, they were an odd personality match. Lee was so controlling. He looked for trouble some days and I was the one who was there and most likely to put up with his rants. Their golden retriever, Sam, the one I saw when I first walked in, seemed to dislike him, too. He would let out this groaning sound and come over to sleep near Chris and me when Lee came around. I'm sure even he tired of Lee's high-pitched, winy voice.

"Okay, John, we need to talk. Follow me to grooming room number one."

He not only said this in his most bitchy tone, but also walked ahead of me like he had a pole up his ass. I followed him with a growing fear I would be tossed to the curb, like a toy that has lost its appeal and is no longer useful. I couldn't understand his power trips. I don't know exactly what I did wrong, but I felt like I couldn't do anything right by him. I was afraid maybe one of his friends or customers didn't like me, and he had changed his minds about hiring me.

"Shut the door, I don't want any customers coming in and overhearing."

I shut the door and felt a pit in my stomach. Maybe this was it, maybe they found out about my eviction or that I lied in my interview. Maybe they found out about my job history or did a background check. Maybe I called Lee out with a look or comment he didn't like. Maybe some of the customers complained about me. Maybe he wanted to get rid of me before I walked out, sensing my irritation with him. It had only been just short of a month I'd been there and things had elevated quickly.

"Here's the deal, John: we need to clean the grooming tubs meticulously with solution after each bath. Chris never does it, but that's why I need to teach you the right way. Now, don't be offended, but Chris' way and my way are very different. Chris has been teaching you his way so far, but my standards are higher than his and I need you to learn my way now."

I felt relieved that this wasn't a termination of employment talk. Suddenly he looked like an acceptable human being. Still a jerk, but I was starting to see that was just his way, and harmless at that. I couldn't let myself take it personally or over-think it.

"Take the spray disinfectant and wash the tub down with a cloth, all knobs too. If one dog is sick and bathes in here, we need to make sure no other dogs are at risk. It's never happened but it's serious stuff and you never know. We don't want to be liable for an outbreak. That's the kind of stuff that could ruin us for good. Chris is too laid back about these things."

He then started to show me by example, vigorously scrubbing while his face became red, concentrating on every nook and cranny while looking up at me to make sure I was paying attention. I wondered if he would get soapy water on his beautiful black clothes, but he didn't.

He then handed me the rag and spray and told me to practice, as he did, cleaning anything that I, or the dogs, might touch. As I did he watched me from near the door. Then I felt him go to the sink and wash his hands before he came up behind me and put his hand on my back, gently sliding his palm up to my shoulder before letting go. It was almost nonchalant and lasted all but two seconds, but it was unsettling. He was trying to test my boundaries and I felt my face flush as I continued to work, my heart beating through my chest.

"Good. You do a good job, John. I'm happy to have you here. We're happy to have you here."

I was nervous, but managed to reply, "Thanks. Happy to be here, Lee."

I didn't want him to hear my voice trembling or see my discomfort. That's what he wanted. He knew that he scared me, and he knew that I'd take it even if it got me angry, which it did. I don't think he cared but for his own amusement. But, I had to tell myself to put up with it, for the sake of a good job. As he left the room, I worried that Chris had returned from lunch and might have seen a glimpse of what happened through the door window. I had no reason to worry, but I did. Lee was attracted to me from the start and I always felt it. It was why he loved demeaning me. The last thing I wanted was for Chris to see me as a threat. Chris is the only breath of fresh air in this place, apart from the dogs.

When I walked out of the room I saw Chris was back and he looked over at me from the desk with slight suspicion. He probably saw Lee walk out a minute before.

It was nearing the end of the day, so I took Bella out for a quick walk, just the two of us. The sun was still out and it was warm. I lay down on the ground while she sat panting at my feet.

'What if I just take her home right now, and never go back to work?' It was a passing thought, a dream. She must have read my thoughts, because she got up and started nudging my face, as if to say, 'yes, take me home.'

Sometimes I wanted to share this with Sara, or have someone to talk to about it all. My life has turned into an ironic comedy, the dogs, Chris and Lee, Bella, the cold showers I took at home, the electric kettle water I shaved with. It would make for a few laughs with someone. I've ended up in some unexpected situations, but this tops the list. Sara would have loved to witness this change, and she would have laughed, too. She would have been impressed seeing me with Bella. But neither she nor anyone else is here to see it. And I know she'd never give me another chance. It dawned on me that I ruined that relationship singlehandedly, and the more time went by, the more I missed and thought of her.

Who knows how I will feel or where I will be in a week, a month, a year from now. All I know is that for the first time in a long time I feel like I am getting somewhere, if that makes any sense. This time will be different. This time I will be patient. I'm not just walking aimlessly these days. I am learning. The last thing I want to be is oblivious.

As I brought Bella back to the shop to get picked up, we stopped around the corner entrance. I hugged her and, without thinking, said to her that she'd be my dog forever no matter what. I don't know why, but I was caught up in the moment and it felt good. Crazy. Here I was talking to a dog and it felt more real than talking to a human.

After work I walked 40 blocks to the subway, just because. The weather was mild for the beginning of March. I didn't know for sure what day it was. At least it was sunny and almost spring.

I had been working at Uptown Dogs for close to a month. Any day, if not today, I was supposed to be out of the apartment, and every day I was relieved to find the locks hadn't yet been changed as scheduled. I always carried a backpack with my basic necessities, which wasn't much, just in case the day came when I wasn't home to grab anything. I knew a way through the back window to get more of my stuff if needed. It's close enough to summer, just a few more touch-and-go months. I can sleep in the park now, Central Park. I must sleep in the park, as there is no other choice and I can't think of another place I know better or that is more convenient for work. I refuse to stay in a shelter. I had no other plan apart from the streets.

So I walked. I took a break from my thoughts, looked around, and thought of some better times in my life.

When I got on the train heading to Brooklyn, I felt someone gently place their hand on my shoulder.

"Hey, John, thought it was you from the back. Long time no see."

I looked at him and shook his hand. Knew the face but the name took longer.

"Frank!" I finally remembered, "I don't believe it! How you been? Thought you moved to Cali or something."

"Arizona," he corrected. "It's beautiful there, but couldn't find steady work, so I'm back here doing construction again."

"Wow...nice. Been so long it took me a second to register." I didn't know what else to say.

"It's great to see you, man. Really."

"You still in Crown Heights with your girl? What's her name again? Pretty with red hair?"

"Ha, Sara," I said. "No, she made a run for it a few weeks back. Finally smartened up."

He was shaking his head looking at me, laughing.

"Oh, well. Trial and error." he said.

"You with the same girl? Rachel?" I asked.

"Yea, actually, we got married last year, got a one-year-old boy and another one on the way. Thirty-nine years old and I have my first kid. Better late than never!"

"Good for you, that's awesome. Congratulations. I get off at the next stop but we should keep in touch. You still got the same number? I got you in my contacts."

"Still do, same number. What are you doing for work these days?" he asked.

"Walking and grooming dogs at this place uptown. It's not so bad. Been there about a month now." As I said this I got shy and started to look around as I spoke, knowing his reaction to come, knowing it would be a surprise for him to hear.

"You kidding me?" He was laughing out loud and I knew this was what I'd get. I was laughing now, too. He thought I was joking for a second and, when he saw I wasn't, his face settled to a smile.

"Hey, the money's green. I'm sure it's better than working with people. I like dogs better, anyway."

"I could use some extra dough, if you know anyone that's looking." When I said this I realized I didn't want to leave the dogs and I didn't have the time, but it came out anyway.

"We could always use a few hands at the site. I can ask. Send me a text so I got your number and I'll keep you posted."

"I'd like that. Thanks a lot, pal."

"Johny, it's really good to see you. Was thinking about you hoping you were okay, especially after that fatso fired you. We all know you broke your back there. It wasn't fair. I remember we used to laugh our asses off…they had to separate us…remember that? We sure had some good times. It's not fun anymore like it used to be, just a bunch of punks working, acting like they know everything. All the good ones moved up or left."

"Nothing's fun like it used to be." And how true it was, even though I muttered it as a mindless response.

Drawing nearer to my stop, I asked, "Still living in Brooklyn?"

"Yeah, I'm still in Brooklyn. Give me a call sometime. Like I said, same number as always. We'll see if we can get you some work. You should come over sometime and see Rachel and the baby."

"Absolutely. I'd love that."

"Yep, see ya later, buddy." I gave his arm a pat and made my way off the train through the rush hour crowd.

Seeing Frank reminded me that I have friends, even if I never saw them. It reminded me of my days working construction and how things were so good back then, but I didn't know it. I was always complaining, thinking there was something else out there that was better, when I had it pretty good.

At home in the hallway facing my door I saw the Sheriff's notice staring right back at me. It was late and I was supposed to be out a week ago, maybe more. I knew the doors were locked but I tried them anyway. Yep, locked. Today was the day and I had a feeling it would be. I went around the back and climbed the fire escape to the back window. The window lock was broken, so I knew I could take one last look inside.

It felt creepy to walk in and sneak around like an intruder. The difference a day can make is not always a good thing. Now I had to tiptoe, grab what I could, and say goodbye. I still couldn't believe the electricity hadn't shut off yet. My bones were cold and sore from walking for so long and I only just felt it as I entered the warmth. In the bedroom I went through the dresser drawers to see if there was something I needed. The bottom drawer had old pictures, change, old IDs, socks, a few letters Sara and I had written to one another after fights, and early love letters we would leave each other on the table before work when she first moved in. I sat down to read them and found myself holding in the heartache that surfaced. It's easy to forget the love you once shared with someone unless you draw upon physical objects, pictures, letters, and other proof of what was dismissed in hostility. I had grown so tired of her and our drab life that I didn't remember this time. She was everything to me back then. There were a few old pictures in frames and our faces looked so full and happy. But in every picture I looked closed up, tense, her arms always around me, yet mine always in front and never returning her embrace. I looked afraid. She was right about me being a shell. I was like that with her from the start, but now I couldn't understand why, because she looked so perfect to me in these photos. I must have thought she wasn't good enough, as a way to shield letting her in. Her fatal flaw was that she loved me more than I loved her, and for that I took her for granted and lost interest. We were very attached, but I still don't know if it was real. It could have been, it could have worked, but it didn't. I wasn't ready.

    I let myself lie back on the bed and, before I knew it, I fell asleep. The blankets were so soft against my face. They still smelled of Sara.

    When I woke it was dark, and I had to pull myself away with all my might and face the certainty of hardship. And, now I cannot look back. It hurts too much to even say goodbye, so I walk through the place looking straight ahead at my exit, avoiding the feelings of loss that have repeatedly broken me. I take what I can and go back out the window and down the fire escape, trying to desensitize myself to the difficulty of an ending, once more.

    And so it begins, I keep saying to myself. I've been waiting for this moment of ultimate collapse all my life and knew it was coming. I contemplated trying to stay the night, but I was worried the landlord or super would come check to it out. I didn't want to risk being woken up like that, possibly arrested. Maybe from this point I can finally find the courage to build myself.

BARE

A month later, needless to say, my life transformed more than I'd ever expected, more than it ever had in such a short amount of time. Living on the streets was greater than a shock and a struggle. It was the dark side of the moon, the darkest side, where you gasp for air and light and try to crawl back to earth. You see stuff in that park you couldn't imagine existed, beyond nightmares. The other night it looked as though a huge beast was running around screaming, but I couldn't focus my eyes enough to see what it really was. I was terrified he would rob me, beat me, maim me, rape me, eat me. You hear screams, whispers, shrieks, voices singing, feet thumping the earth beneath you, critters scurrying around, shady deals gone bad, babies being born, people being killed, assaulted, beaten, and the world ending. Even my sweet dreams have turned on me.

Your mind plays tricks on you, and what you see and hear plays tricks on your mind. All your dreams are in the park, but it's not the same park. It's a different dimension that others can't see. It's play land for the spirits of Central Park past and present, reliving their horrors, forcing you in through their realm to see their sad story play out over and over. Sometimes they grab your hand and try to take you with them, while you are unable to speak, move, wake, and fight them off. I can never make out their faces, but they always have dark features, and there are always lights flashing in the distance before they arrive.

The dreams and the spirits can swallow you up and take you way on the other side, as though you were never born, as though this reality is only a dream from the other side. All the sounds you hear play a role in these dreams, and you can't tell what's real or not, but you're always trying to hide and run.

And there is no escape. Home is an illusory place to me

now. The people that seem crazy to the rest of the world are just people who have seen this side more than the other. It's a circus, a freak show, a frightening movie, and half of them aren't even people. They are creatures, insects, reptiles, demons, animals, ghosts, spirits, aliens, and other indistinguishable life.

There is no adjusting. It scarred me like nothing else I'd ever been through, mostly because I was so lost and cold, near frozen when it was windy. If it were January or February I would have died out here. I barely got any sleep. The first night I saw and felt someone in a big black hoodie reach down towards me and grip my throat while I tried to move his arm, for what felt like minutes, only to wake alone in my own breathlessness. There was no face, just a big black hole.

If only someone would take me by the arm and bring me home, let me rest, feed me, let me stay to recuperate, and let this all be over. If only this could be like one of those stories where a priest or someone forgiving bestows kindness on me. Everything hurts. My heart is broken from it all, shattered. Worse than if a woman broke it. It was broken from life, from people, from feeling bare and dirty, broken from trying to find a path up but spiraling down. Broken from waking up to rats crawling around and pigeon shit on me. Broken from trying to avoid the other dwellers that try to clock me to see if they can rob me. Broken from seeing those who have lost their minds and afraid I can intimately understand how they got there. Broken from not being able to trust myself. Broken from people walking by looking at me as though I were sub human. To them, I am just some byproduct of modern society that belonged exactly where I was by my own doing, my own laziness, my own inferiority, my own mental incapacity, and I should be moved to some institution. I don't know if I can argue that, but they are still no better than I am, as far as I'm concerned. And I still want to be here and not cast off elsewhere, just as much as they want to be here.

There is a line to draw between people now; those of us who live out here, and everyone else.

It was hard work hiding my new predicament from Chris and Lee. I became paranoid that they would have an idea, but it was a long shot, unless they walked by me in the park while I was sleeping. Sure, I recycled outfits. I even had a locker I rented at a gym I signed up to where I kept my extra clothes and belongings, so at least I could switch them up when needed, and shower. But it was all within a style I had kept from the beginning. I had the feeling they thought of me as their grungy novelty, and liked to show their friends that they had someone cool working for them.

Every day I opened the shop early, at 6 a.m. I washed up a bit, changed, threw my old clothes in the washer and dryer, took a quick nap, and then opened the doors at 8 a.m. It gave me a chance to charge my phone, brush my teeth, and throw some cold soapy water on my face. Chris and Lee never arrived before 10 a.m., not since giving me the key to open. I started handling the morning drop-off rush by myself. It was good, kept me busy, and gave my life some structure.

I worked as much as I could during the day to keep myself sane. If only it were enough, yet there was still this acute feeling of boredom the moment I left. Having a job and money in my pocket wasn't enough. I wanted off the streets so badly. I wanted to leave work and have somewhere to go and something to do. I wanted to be able to go home to Brooklyn and walk in my apartment and still have all my stuff and bed to sink into. But, most of all, I was so lonely. I wanted someone to be there for me. As unhealthy as the whole situation with Sara had become, in my sad state I would have gone back to it, if it were still an option. Luckily, it wasn't. I knew I needed that chapter to close.

I'd been able to save money for the first time in a while, which made it easier to endure the nights in the park. Money was a safety net, and just to think of having some put aside always made me feel better. It wasn't much, but it had been a long time since the numbers were going up rather than down, and I had very little expenses. Though the more I saved, the cheaper I became. Saving a nickel, a dime, or a quarter became so significant that I was living less than I had to, going out of my way for the cheapest I could find and only allowing myself the minimum. I even became cheaper with people, never leaving tips like I used to, being miserly. Whatever I had to do just to save something, and it became the only control I had left.

I started to make a few friends in the park. Most of them were just 'neighbors' that had seen me around, and began to nod their heads towards me when passing and make small talk. Sometimes I had good conversations with them that lasted late into the night. They are of all different types and backgrounds, and there are more of them than I'd ever noticed before. Some of them I wouldn't know were homeless if I had passed them in the street, while others are obvious. Some are so far gone that there is not talking to them, and some have let their hygiene go to the point where you can't even bear to get close. The park is huge. I cannot imagine how many more of us there are out there.

Babble is the only one that regularly comes around to say 'hi.' His name is Mark, but everyone calls him Babble because he never shuts up, which is true. He can make some normal conversation, but most of what he says is incoherent, and after a few minutes he gets antsy and acts like he has somewhere to run off to, walking away mid sentence. I've told him a million times that I don't smoke and a million times he has asked for a cigarette. Then there are moments he says something accidentally brilliant and I wonder if he's crazy at all, or just playing some joke on all of us. I'd like to believe he is a genius that is entertained by these games he plays, laughing at us all for believing him, probably going back to his Park avenue apartment after he's got his fill. He is always circling the park, asking people for cigarettes that he stuffs in his pockets and never smokes, and trying to collect change from the passing crowds. He is a cricket to me. All he does is walk back and forth chirping.

That first night I wore two sweaters, two pairs of thick socks, and two pairs of thermals under my jeans, which were half the clothes I owned. The jacket was big, heavy, and ugly, from the thrift shop. I bought a blanket and walked around the park with my duffle bag for hours. I expected the worst, yet knew I would get through it. There were possible nooks to sleep in, but I wanted privacy, privacy somewhere unseen and off the path, and that wasn't on a bench. When I found a spot, the ground was so cold. It was emanating through my blanket like ice, and I cried. With no expression the tears rolled down my cheeks in constant succession, like they had all day and would the next. I was afraid someone would see me like that, so I covered my face with my scarf. There was no end to how much I felt I could cry, to the pain, to the indescribable void within me. If ever there was a moment I would have, could have, and possibly should have ended my life, it was then.

I waited for a dream to come, hoping to be tired enough, and I finally was. As a result, someone tried to snatch my backpack from under my head and the sneakers off my feet. But I woke, confused, and they disappeared in a flash, which made me wonder if it was just a dream, a dream playing on my fears like the one before it of being choked. I wondered what was real, and why I distinctly felt someone trying to pull my belongings from me. I wondered where I was. I wondered who I was and why disorientation made me feel like such a stranger to myself.

I was in shock that this was my life, something I would become familiar with eventually, like all other things, if I'm lucky. I couldn't believe that I had sunk to this. The shock was so great that it prevented me from falling back asleep most nights.

And this has been what every night since then has felt like, with a temporary feeling here and there that it wasn't so bad, and a temporary feeling here and there that it couldn't get any worse. When it was good it was almost tolerable, when it was bad it was unbearable. The wind was the real grim reaper of it all.

I couldn't sleep that first night — not after that dream — nor the second, nor the third, or since then. Only a few light minutes or hours here and there. It was hard to tell what sleep was anymore. I felt awake all night, but knew I had slept some, half stuck in that purgatory world of Central Park, half awake and on guard.

There are some druggie alcoholics that hang out not far from where I settle in. I see them coming out after dark and they see me as they drink and smoke their cigarettes, and whatever else they do. I try to avoid eye contact, because I don't want to make any connection. These guys aren't like the others, the old down-and-out bums and lunatics who are stuck out here. These guys are predators. I don't understand why I hate them so much, but I truly do. Many of them look slimy and exactly like the kind of people I don't want to have anything to do with. They are afraid of nothing, they are smart, and they could figure out a way to get me. To do what? I don't know exactly, but whatever it could be, it would put me a lot worse off.

Maybe it was one of them that tried to steal from me that first night. They would try to rob me every night if they could. They huddle in their circles blowing smoke and opening beers, and get louder and louder until the light hours when they disperse. It makes it even harder for me to sleep knowing they are there, seeing and hearing them gets me sick. There is nothing I'm too afraid of losing in my bag. There is nothing of real value I have with me that can't be replaced. At any moment I am willing to fight these losers, because they are the enemy of the little pride and possessions I have left. Or at least I've made them my enemy for the time being. I had become paranoid in my loneliness. I can't discern the difference between which thoughts have truth to them anymore. The truth is always changing in my head, but it's safer not to trust. It's safer to make judgments that maintain my distance.

    Another thing I noticed was how one small day felt so long. So, so long. It felt like I was wasting every second and prolonging every sensation, wasting away my time and energy, yet there was nothing to be done of it. Work was a welcome ten hours, and I was up at sunrise just waiting to go in. Thinking of the dogs, dogs that are running to me and wagging their tails. Those were the thoughts that staved off the depression. I tried to think of their faces as often as I could, as often as redundant and unwelcomed thoughts came into my mind. There was nothing left pleasant to think of, because there was nobody and nothing more in my life. If only I could think of nothing and allow myself to be happy, for once. I thought about getting in touch with Frank since I saw him on the train, but I didn't know what to say. When I get back on my feet, I'll give him a call and meet his baby.

    Sometimes I just sat on a bench, looking ahead and all around me. I couldn't relax my face, the stress was too great, and I found myself leaning forward with my elbows bent on my legs, just trying to stop myself from thinking how it all went wrong. I would sit like this for hours. Trying to stop myself for being ashamed for feeling and acting so weak, when I knew I had been stronger than this in my life.

Every morning at the shop I talked to people that I would never talk to otherwise, people who would look down at me if they saw me sleeping in the park, yet people who seemed delighted to see me as they walked in with their dogs.

After work, I hopped from one warm, public place to the next, mainly coffee shops, avoiding the brisk spring weather. Most the time I'd order a coffee and sandwich, then fall asleep trying to read the paper. My head would bob all over the place as I napped, and sometimes my mouth would hang open and I'd drool. It was the only time I could sleep somewhat safely. I made sure to go to better parts of town and sit in the very back of these places, with my hat on and head down, wearing sunglasses. It was so incredibly draining. I watched people who seemed to be preoccupied with their phones and laptops. The worst part was when the place was near closing and I would have to come to terms with leaving. At least now I had upgraded to sleeping on a bench. Only problem is that it's closer to the junkie crew, but still a better spot than before, under a tree that blocks the early sunlight.

Since a few weeks back I've seen a man doing what I'm doing, day squatting in the same café. No shortage of squatter types in this city. He is old, in his seventies, with a white beard and very dirty hands and clothes. Nobody can sit near him because he smells so bad. The employees talk of how he comes there every day and just stares out the window. People give repulsed looks, but he never sees or cares what is going on around him. The workers don't have the nerve to ask the poor old man to leave, which is the only kindness they indeliberately show him. I wondered how he could have nothing, nowhere to go and nobody to take him in. It could be for any reason, any reason at all. At his age, chances are dried up, nonexistent, gone. I'm sure he knows this, too.

When I saw him last I had this great feeling of empathy,

because I now share a sliver of his experience. He bends over a coffee and his head leans forward, his eyes scan the room and table, then he reaches for a paper and places it flat in front of him. When he starts to read his eyes begin to close, and the process repeats for as long as it can until he is sound asleep. In this café, there are all these clean-cut looking people. The kind who would complain if they didn't get the coffee drink they wanted, the apartment they wanted, the irresistible person they wanted, the job they wanted, or if they realized they didn't know everything like they thought they did. The kind of people who don't realize what they have, and judge others. And then there is this guy, who looks so out of place, like an ant they would crush if they could get away with it, and they could. I bought him two sandwiches and left them by his coffee as he slept with his head forward. It eased my conscience, and for that it was selfish. If I had more to give, I'd give it. I would hope someone would do the same for me one day, if needed.

  I never saw him return to the café after that day. Maybe he died. Maybe he migrated to another café. Maybe he was in an institution, or had a home to go back to. Maybe my show of charity upset him and was a sign for him to move on. I feared I would end up like he him. He is real, but he is also a mirror, a vision of what might be my future self, and he crossed my path to show me something. I wanted to avoid his state at all costs.

And I thought of him often.

*****

Friday night, and I'm in the 24-hour McDonald's. It's been one of those days that just won't end. At least McDonald's is easy. They have no standards. I can sleep in there and nobody will kick me out or notice me. And I just might sleep here all night to avoid the rain outside. I'd rather stay in this plastic seat under the fluorescent lights than under the full moon. I'll find more places to hop around to tomorrow, but for now it is here, and I don't want to move for a while. I can't move. My body and brain are aching for rest. It has been cold and rainy all week, and it's taken its toll.

There is a young black kid sitting across from me. We're the only ones upstairs and he knows I'm here to sleep, nothing more. I am no threat to him. I know what he's up to because I've seen him here before doing just what he is doing now, dealing drugs — conspicuously. A few people come up to see him and they play this game where the money slips from one hand, drugs to the other, as if they're shaking hands, but it's obvious. Anyone can clearly see what is really happening, because he always looks at the money under the table before he spits a bag into his hand after. He keeps looking at me when the transaction happens, watching my eyes and constantly checking to make sure I don't seem too interested in what he's doing.

I don't know how long it was that I fell asleep with my head on the table, but I woke to a sound that has no good possibilities. I jumped off the seat and I looked up, still completely deaf from the blast.

"Who's looking tough now? You can't talk now, can you, bitch?! Should have paid me my money!"

My heart was beating so fast that I couldn't believe I heard anything after that. Another young black kid stood over the drug dealer with a gun pointed down at him. There was blood pouring out from his underside. All I could do was bury my head in my folded arms before me and hope I wasn't next. Barely breathing. I peeked up in curiosity.

The dealer was still alive, gurgling on his own blood from a stomach shot. I watched as, in shock, he seemingly tried to make sense of it all. He was dying, and his eyes fixed on the ceiling without acknowledgment of the person over him, only that he was facing death. I closed my eyes and nestled my head in my arms on the table once more, fearful the killer would notice me. I heard him laugh. He stepped over the corpse and walked over to me.

'This is it. I'm gonna die like this, sitting in a McDonald's, cursing the day I came to this stinking city.'

"That's right, ya bum, keep your fucking eyes and mouth shut or I'll come find your dirty, smelly ass and give you what I gave him."

Then he walked away. I glanced at him briefly as he ran down the stairs and out. He had a bandana covering his face, and a cap on so low that you could barely make out his eyes. He looked like anyone else his type, was dressed like anyone else his type, talked like anyone else his type. The place went completely silent. They'll never find him. Black stuff; drug stuff; street stuff; poor people stuff; unsophisticated crime stuff; cops don't care about him any more than they care about me.

My first reaction was to run out of there, but my quivering legs drew me to the body. I stood over the dealer and wondered if there was something I could do for him. When I knelt down his eyes moved to meet mine, and it looked like he made a great effort to do so. There was so much blood that I kept worrying it would get on my clothes or stain the bottoms of my sneakers, but as I hopped my feet over to avoid the puddle, I grabbed his hand. I wasn't sure why. I think my mouth opened to speak but nothing came out, no question I could think of, no closing words for him. His eyes looked like that of a scared animal and I saw that he was about to go, he was drifting and giving up his fight. Blood was coming out of his mouth and he started choking on it. He was just a kid. He didn't know any better. Just go, whoever you are. I hope you get to start over in another life. Another life where you have better chances. He clenched my hand as he looked at me, but I'm not sure he knew what he was doing.

In this instant, I felt envious of him. Envious that already he could see something beyond what I could see. Envious that he didn't waste away before he died, like the old man in the café would — or had. Envious that someone had spared him impending doom while still in his prime.

There was an air that exited him, and then he was stiff, staring at me still, but with blank doll eyes. He looked as innocent as a child. My heart was still pounding so loud, but I knew to get up and leave as fast as I could. The cops would take at least 20 minutes. People were looking up the staircase, their clamoring growing louder and louder, but when they saw me start down they quieted. A voice called out,

"Is it safe to go up there?"

"Yep. He's gone." I replied.

"What do you mean by that?"

I didn't answer. I didn't know what I really meant or who I was talking about, the killer or the victim, but they'd find out soon enough. Two addicts scaled the stairs and a manager yelled at them to stop, but they didn't. They wanted to steal whatever drugs they could before the cops showed up. They were next in line to buy. Now, he's one less dealer to feed the self-destruction in this world.

When the crowd saw me coming, they parted, and the store managers ran up after the junkies. I heard one of them say, "Oh shit," as he reached the top. Everyone was muttering, "what happened?" and "did someone get shot?" They were so excited by the death and wanted gossip. It was like they cared more about the sensation of it all than for the life that was lost. They'd probably take pictures if they could, selfies even. They were on their phones, calling to spread the news and be the 100th person to call 9-1-1. I heard a loud, "Hey, grab him!" coming from the manager upstairs. When I heard that I ran right through the doors, around the corner through an alley and kept running. My ears were still ringing, but I didn't hear sirens, so I kept going until I was far away.

  I didn't feel like answering questions or being a witness. I didn't feel like giving a description of the killer. I didn't feel like admitting to napping in McDonald's and having the cops view me as the bum bystander, or answering questions about who I am, where I work and live, and where I'm from. Playing cool, I walked to the park. No cop car ever passed me and I was, like the killer, a needle in a haystack, just an anonymous person in the streets of New York City. The paradox of what is at once grand and grotesque about this city. I didn't want to deal with it. Any one of us could be a normal person, a killer, or both, but make no mistake; none of us in this place are without some kind of pathology. I couldn't sleep after that.

  Light rain felt refreshing as it came down. My eyes could barely blink from feeling wired. I walked and walked, searching for some place to rest. I knew once I stopped my mind would rehearse the event over and over. There was nothing to sway me from thinking these things, and somehow being outside in the open air lessened the brutality of it all. I was worried I'd get blamed, or that the cops would be looking for me. There was a chance it could happen, albeit slim, but I can't be sure it wouldn't. I could be an easy target and a scapegoat, if one was needed.

  Alcohol was the only answer. It had been a while since I drank, but I was willing to try anything that was quick. For the first time in a long time, I went to the liquor store and bought a liter of cheap vodka, opening it right on the sidewalk and drinking it all the way back into the park. It hit me fast. I remember this feeling. I'd become a lush in these past few years that I barely drank. The cheap stuff, it tasted like rubbing alcohol and felt like fire in my belly. It was hard to swallow, but after a few seconds I acclimated.

And the more I drank, the better and worse I felt.

I watched people watch me watching them. Tourists moved their eyes over to me as I staggered through the streets with my now half-empty bottle. I felt rebellious, and had drunken outbursts of laughing and talking to myself. A desperate man I am. How easy it is to become desperate. How easy it is to lose footing. How easy it is to begin to slip, trying to hold on to the little one has in life when there is so little to lose. It all goes so fast, like whiplash, and leaves us bewildered of the how, what, and why. How hard it is, for all of us. How did it end up like this for me? It is supposed to be like this. I willed this to be so, for some purpose. I need to tell myself there is a plan for all of this, but I'm not so sure I still believe there is a plan for anything at all.

These people I see walking by, they are lucky. I'd like to sleep in their beds, be kissed by their women, live the life they are so stupidly ungrateful to have, while they complain about ridiculousness. They think I'm a fool, but they are bigger slaves than me.
I'm wasted, and not responsible for my actions tonight.

"Her eyes they shone like the diamonds, you'd think she was queen of the land. Her hair hung over her shou-oolders, tied up with a black velvet bannd..."

It was an old Irish song my father used to come home singing when he was drunk. I never forgot the words. Passersby sometimes laughed, and sometimes ran away clutching their children close, shielding them from the sight of me, prepared to cover their ears, avert their eyes, or raise their fists.

I completely forgot the earlier events of the night, as intended. I felt good. Too good. I wanted more alcohol before I finished the bottle I was holding. I was afraid I would lose the feeling too fast, that this excitement would disappear, leaving me more dismal than usual. And it would. I didn't want to be dropped from this momentous high. My bench is a far, far way down that I don't want to be reminded of.

But I didn't move, because I wasn't sure I wanted more just yet. I wasn't sure if I wanted to have a huge hangover and possibly wake with my stuff stolen from passing out. So I sat, took baby sips from the remainder of the bottle, and got a pack of cigarettes that I chain-smoked and lost somewhere on my route. Then I headed to my bench; it was quiet on the path. I felt like going out to a club or bar to keep the night going, but another part of me felt like throwing up and calling it a night. I kept telling myself to end this already, just be done with it. Forget the casualties of the night, it comes with the territory; there was nothing special about the black kid — or any of us. We all die. It's a favor that some of us go sooner and swifter than others. Especially if you've got a crappy life like him and end up dealing drugs in McDonalds.

As I walked, I began to regret tonight deeply. I started to feel so down. There was an echo of silence that rung all around me. It was loneliness, such crippling loneliness, after such loud chaos. And there was nothing I could do about it.

While being drunk I had a profound revelation about my life and who I am. It altered me enough to get perspective, to arrive at a truth, if only this truth could be remembered the next day to be useful. What good can it do? I don't know. I saw myself from a distance. I saw someone who was sitting back letting life happen. The thought of this resulted in my polishing off the remainder of the bottle in two gulps, hoping that the silence would go away once more and I would die in my sleep, wake up into a better dream, or die from this dream and wake up into a better life.

When I wake tomorrow, I vow there will be a change. I

don't know what kind of change, but something. Others, worse off than me, have changed. I could think of the old man in the café as a catalyst. My fear of becoming like him could be enough to fuel me, or enough for me to pull the trigger. That's why I could never forget his face, because it was traumatic and effective at the same time. I still don't know how his memory would play out in my life, if it would.

My eyes weren't seeing straight, but I could smell the druggie alcoholics were out. Call it a sixth sense, or just the knowledge that they were always out at this time. The regular lurkers and creepers and a few more I didn't recognize. I sat there on my bench, head back and hiccupping, looking up to find they were all staring at me from across the way. This changed any notions they may have entertained about my being a 'clean', 'stuck-up' bum.

And, just like that, it happened. In my drunken state I made conversation, or they made conversation, and I stumbled over to them, or they stumbled over to me. I can't remember. I was so dizzy and gone. We started talking and, next thing I knew, I was holding a pipe and took a hit of whatever it was. Someone lit it and I inhaled, holding it in for a few seconds before releasing. It could have been anything. I was so drunk I couldn't tell. The smoke came out like steam from a bull's nostrils. It killed the booze instantly. It killed my misery instantly.

They asked me questions about what my deal was and I answered them all honestly. No need to lie around people like this, they didn't care and were unable to shock. I was surprised they wanted to know about me, so I told them about Sara and the eviction, and how I ended up out here. They told me that this old guy had occupied the bench I had been sleeping on. It was his bench, so to speak, but he died of a heart attack the day before I grabbed it. Apparently it was a prime bench for park dwellers. I wondered for a second if it was the old man from the café.

No. Couldn't be.

Most of them were city guys. The strong accents gave them away. This one short guy sitting on the bench rolling a cigarette caught my attention. He had a pug nose and brown hair. His body was that of a midget, with legs and arms that looked shorter than his torso. He was wearing these funny Wrangler jeans pulled up high and had no shoelaces in his filthy sneakers. I laughed to myself when I saw him talking. He had one tooth in the front, maybe more in the back that I couldn't see, and when he smoked he blew the smoke out of his mouth like he was whistling and went right back to his story, holding the cigarette between his forefinger and thumb by his face. Another one was wearing a rope in place of a belt in his jeans and had his legs crossed, listening to the story and trying very hard to look awake. Not all of them were sloppy looking. Some were dressed in clean looking athletic outfits, and many of them were wearing caps either forward or backward, and some even looked like funky artistic types. After my prior distrust of them, I felt comfortable here now. They all looked like characters, but the kind you don't read about in stories. Nobody could make this stuff up.

I had a long talk with a few of the more normal looking guys. One of them was talking about his service days in the Middle East and every time he finished his sentence, I would forget what he said. We were all so high, and I didn't even know what I was saying or if I made any sense. That was a sign for me to take it easy.

There were about fifteen of us standing around. A guy named Tony told stories from when he used to be a whale of a cocaine dealer up in the Bronx. He had slicked back black hair, pock marked cheeks, and hazel eyes. His clothes were cool and he looked put-together for the most part. I'd seen him around before and always thought he looked shady, but I was wrong. He's not so bad. I don't know what he was saying, but I know it was funny and interesting. He kept looking at me as he spoke, maybe because the other guys were half-listening, or maybe because he wanted to impress me because I was new. His Puerto Rican accent was amusing. And he was animated telling his stories, reenacting them, throwing his hands and arms about as he spoke, speaking in different voices, and asking us questions like, "And what do you think happened next?" The rest of us watched, some guys starting their own conversations, and others interjecting to add to the stories he told. There were a lot of, 'Yea I remember that time, Tony.' And 'We really got fucked up that time.'

When Tony finished, he sat next to where I had sat on the top part of the bench. He asked how long I'd been sleeping on the streets, and if anyone had snagged my kicks or anything else. Nobody had, I told him, though it happens at least once to everyone here. These thieves prowl around at night and somehow get away with slipping sneakers right off the feet of sleeping people. Those who already have nothing to their name wake up with even less. Everyone always asks me this question and is surprised mine haven't been stolen…yet.

For hours we all sat on these benches and shot the shit, talking about money, the city, jail, girls, stories of who knew who, who did what, getting high, gambling, hustling, and other random stuff. I wasn't so different from these guys, even though I didn't have anything like their stories to contribute. Nothing of the drug or criminal sort, but I was fine listening. I felt comfortable, because I knew they weren't the types to think about what anyone else was doing and they didn't have any requirements. They were unaffected.

My body had taken a beating and it was catching up to me, but mentally I was calm. The drugs and alcohol had all but worn off. If I were alone right now, I would have definitely been depressed.

Hours passed without feeling the time. The sun started coming up and the guys dispersed. Usually I witnessed their end of night, early morning departure from my bench upon waking, but this time I didn't notice. Like flies they disappeared in different directions, until just a couple of us remained. In the light, our faces emerged, our 5 o'clock shadows, our hollows eyes, our grimy hair, our giant pupils, and our ruddy cheeks, red from windburn. I knew I looked as rough as they did. For once I wasn't aware what people walking by thought of us, not the early morning runners, or the tourists. I used to be embarrassed to be seen sleeping out here by civilians. Not only was I not aware of it, I didn't care.

"Tony, you sleep in the park, too?" I asked.

"Well, I've done it, just like you, man. Just like you, I been doing it in the cold, wearing everything I had, smelling bad, washing myself in public restrooms. Not anymore. I got a little place of my own these days."

"Yeah," I replied, nodding. "Hopefully it won't be long before I find a spot, too. Just recovering from some tough times, but I'll be back on my feet soon."

I wasn't sure if getting back on my feet was a reality. I wasn't sure I'd ever really been on my feet to begin with. But, I hoped I wouldn't be in this godforsaken park forever.

"You got a job though, right? Mikey seen you walking dogs for those two fags. Do they know you're sleeping out here?"

I was scared that they already knew too much about me. They were keeping tabs on me, knew where I worked, knew of Chris and Lee. It might not have been on purpose that they did, but it still took me by surprise and Tony sensed it.

"We only noticed because we thought you might be a cop, that's all. Saw you with the dogs one day walking out of there. Seemed clear you weren't, but you look a little more put together than the guys who usually end up sleeping out here."

It was quiet for a minute. I didn't answer his question, so he asked again.

"Those guys know you sleeping out here?"

"No. Not that I know of. They ain't so bad. And, no, I'm definitely no cop."

"That dog parlor you work in used to be a liquor store back in the day. You could walk in the back and play craps, launder money in the basement, or you could go upstairs and play high stakes card games. Now I walk by and see those two you work for and I can't get used to it. Don't get me wrong, it's a good thing, but I've seen this place change so much over the years. It's crazy. That place and those two are a reminder of what's happening around here. This is not the New York City I remember."

"It's a far cry from that now. I'm there for the dogs and the money and that's all. I wouldn't be uptown if I weren't working there. Never thought I'd end up on a park bench like this, but every day I'm glad I got that job."

"Man, I love dogs so much. Used to have a pit bull. He got sick and I couldn't afford to get him fixed up, so I had to leave him with the vet. I still feel like it's my fault, like I could have prevented it, but I just hope he got better and someone took him home. Just hope they didn't put him down. There was no way to know, and I didn't have the heart to call and find out. I keep telling myself he's in some nice home upstate with a family and a big backyard, running around with some doggy friends."

Tony looked sad, and I heard it in his voice. I just looked ahead. We were sitting on the top of the bench still, watching the sun peeking up over the buildings. I felt sick and tired, but couldn't stop watching the sun. Thinking how beautiful it all is on this day that I'm not waking alone.

There was something about Tony I really liked. He was mellow, seemed to know everything about everything in this city. The more I talked to him, the more I felt he had one of the most interesting personalities of anyone I'd ever met. He was smart enough to do whatever he wanted if he actually had the inclination. But something told me he likes his life just the way it is, that he has no second thoughts about it, and he doesn't care what anyone says or thinks about it. It never occurred to me that I could do the same.

I didn't want to go to sleep and I was sure that I couldn't if I tried. I had almost forgotten about the scene in McDonald's, and to think of it momentarily made me shudder. On top of coming down, I was already drudging to get through the day ahead. It was fully light now, and my body was feeling the lack of sleep.

I had no clue how I would recover from it all, but I knew I wanted to stay with Tony. To be alone would be devastating. Heartbreaking even. I could tell Tony didn't want to be alone either, because he had chances to go but was still hanging around talking, about himself — seemed that's what he liked to do most. And I liked it too. I didn't care how much of it was true or not. I can only imagine that he's seen a lot more than he lets on or can remember, and that there are a lot more stories he'll probably never repeat.

We walked around the park for a while and exited at Columbus Circle. All of a sudden, I remembered the spectacle I made there last night and was sickened to think of it. No more hard alcohol for a while. Tony brought me to a bodega that sold $1 coffee and cheap forty ounce bottles of beer. We grabbed one of each and he then said he had no money, so I paid for his. He had money, though. I saw the outline of bills in his back pocket with a corner of one popping out the top. Then he asked if I could buy him some smokes. He was generous with me the night before, so I agreed. It wasn't a big deal.

On a bench back in the park again, he talked more. This time he spoke about his family while he took turns drinking from both the coffee and the beer. He spoke of his mother in Puerto Rico and how he was going to see her soon, and finally settle down there. Said he missed her but just couldn't get his shit together to get on a plane. He also said his brother and sisters live in the Bronx and hate him, hadn't seen them in ages. His sister tried to call the cops on him last time he showed up at her house, and accused him of trying to steal her wedding ring. No doubt there was some truth to that story. When he spoke of his mother, he looked in the distance at the trees and pond before where we sat, like he was seeing her in his mind.

"She's got over thirty animals in the house with the cats and dogs, and a bunch of birds outside. All of them are from the street or dumped on her doorstep, some of them were abused so bad and she had to take them to the vet to get stitched up. She's got a heart of gold, and it's crazy all the work she does just to keep it up. I should be down there helping her out, instead I'm up here, doing, well, god knows what. I don't even know why I'm still here, chasing my own tail."

My eyes were fixed upon him as he talked. I remembered the day I first saw him and thought what a low person he seemed, and now he looked sincere and real. It made me realize how unfair I was to vilify him, and how judgmental I had become in my defensive state.

"I can get clean, but I always eventually relapse. You name it, I've done everything from A to Z. It's mostly booze and pills but I still have nasty bouts with the hard drugs here and there. It's the best I can do. One of these days I'll get on a plane and surprise my mom and just start over, clean and sober. One of these days real soon. I can feel it's coming. I'll be gone in a flash with just the clothes on my back. Poof."

He made a motion with his hand cupped in the shape of a circle, like he was blowing smoke through it the same way he'd disappear.

"There's nothing legit you want to do or get here?" I asked.

He looked startled at the idea of wanting anything, of reality, of wanting to fit into this society, of an alternative life, just as I was. What was there for people like us to do here anyway? That shock never goes away, because there are no guarantees, not in the moment or in the future, to any of our efforts. People like us barely try, we are inconsistent, we don't qualify, and we know we can't please or compete. Everyone always gets sick of us and we expect that. But, we have that back-up plan to go home someday, because we know mom is always there for us. Just the thought of being responsible for anyone or anything is panic, and nobody understands the way we think. We float on the fringes in life. It is constant wandering and wondering that only gets more difficult, yet tapers off at the same time.

"You play the cards you get dealt. That's that. I don't sit around dwelling on stupid shit no more, shit I'm never gonna get or do. I'm not trying to be a square. This is my life and I'm happy with it. I've seen a lot more than the average person out there. If I die tomorrow, I wouldn't have any regrets. And, boy, do I got some stories..hahaha..I could fill a book."

He looked at me with an expression that said he had accepted himself. At least he's got his pride. He chose this life. Even though he is telling me, in other words, that he has just given up. I don't know the difference between going the way you have to go or going the way you want, between choosing or being stuck, trying and quitting, and for him it's all the same. Maybe that's all that's important, not fighting it. Not thinking about it. Not complaining about it. Being unattached, just letting it happen, and being yourself. I need to get to that state of mind. I only know what I'm told by someone who fools me into thinking they know better, who fools me into thinking I should have something everyone else wants, too. I don't know who I'd be if I knew how to let myself go. I still have an impulse to chase something, and I need to give up on that like he has.

Could I tell stories like he does? I doubt it. I'd never have stories like that. Tony was too intelligent, too funny, and too talented at nothing in particular.

"Don't know about you, kid, but I'm spent. I've been up for three nights running and I gotta hit the sack. What about you? What's your plan?"

"Try to sleep, too, I guess."

"Here?"

"Yep, we passed my bench back there. Well, you know."

"Yea, kid, I know where you sleep, just didn't know if you were going to work or what."

"It's Saturday. They're closed today." I replied.

He looked around as though he were thinking of something. I could tell he wanted to help me out, he had a heart, and would think of a way it would benefit him, which would make me feel more comfortable. There is nothing I hate more than a handout.

"Okay, here's the story: I don't know you, but you seem like a solid guy — you got a job and you're clean for the most part. I got a couch you can sleep on if you pay me twenty bucks a night…we'll see how it goes from tonight, no promises, but I could use the money. You could be out of the cold and get some sleep."

It was worth a try, and I was looking forward to sleeping on a couch. He mentioned nothing of the money I just spent on his coffee, beer and cigs, but it didn't matter, the offer was worth a lot more to me than that. I got everything in the bank and had nothing but clothes, hygiene items, and blankets in my bag, so there was nothing he could want or get. And there was something in it for both of us. It was nice of him to offer; most people would never do that. I was floored by his generosity, a rare thing in this city. Before I answered him I paused, in an attempt to hide seeming overly enthusiastic at the thought of resting somewhere safe.

"I'd really appreciate that, thank you. It would help for sure to sleep on a couch other than the bench."

"It's nothing," he smiled. And with that we got up, walked to the train, and headed to Spanish Harlem. We were both worn out. We spoke little but made a few comments here and there how we were hurting to crash. Tony updated me on some of the guys that were there the night before with us. He said that some of them were cool but the rest were sketchy, that I should watch out, never give them any money or anything, and never tell them too much about myself. He said they were the kind of guys who'd steal my wallet then help me look for it.

Tony's place was tiny, and a mess; two rooms in a dump basement in a dump building. It looked like a space that a building super would live in. There were a few windows looking out on passing feet on the sidewalk. Fortunately, it was warm, because the furnace was close behind another door in the main basement. I was still so cold from being out all night that I didn't take my jacket off.

The place smelled, reeked, like cigarettes, stale beer, and rotten food. The walls and ceilings had brown water stains all over them and there was a light bulb hanging from above, covered in cobwebs, which he turned on. It looked even worse in the light, and that means a lot coming from me, because I have lived in one or two shitholes in my day. But, in spite of my shock, I told him, while scaling the walls with wide eyes, that it wasn't so bad.

He looked at me surprised, his head fell back and his knees bent for a second while loudly laughing.

"Don't give me that bullshit. Either you're lying though your teeth or you've been living in the tunnels. This place is a rat nest. Even I know that. I'm gonna clean and make it nice one of these days, maybe next week."

I looked at him and we laughed, "Yeah, I'm just trying be nice. It's a fuckin' dump, all right, but it's warm and it's something, and I'm grateful to you, man. I'll help you clean it."

He put a blanket on the couch for me and went into his room. I saw it was small and messy and dark, just a twin bed, some folding chairs, a nightstand, clothes strewn about, baseball caps hanging on nails on the wall, scattered broken electronics, and trash. I sat on the couch, which looked like a pack of dogs tore apart. The flowery pink and brown fabric was ripped and the filling from the cushions was everywhere, springs coming out, cigarette burns. It smelled like a bar and had booze stains all over it. Then I laughed, because I couldn't help but find it all comical. He saw me and knew why I did; he knew this place was a trip.

There was an old television covered in dust in the corner. He turned it on for a second, adjusting the foil bunny ears he'd made as the antenna. He then pointed to the bathroom and kitchen and said that the grand tour could be seen from where I sat. The television barely came in, but you could make out a rerun of Taxi. To the left of me I observed a small bathroom with a door that looked like window shutters, a toilet, a tiny sink, and a shower with a dirty curtain that was half hanging on. The linoleum floors were peeling and rotting. I went to the bathroom and noticed the absolute filth and scum covering all surfaces. I'm no clean freak, but I had a strong urge to take a fire hose of bleach and boiling water to the place — even a sandblaster or, hell, maybe just a match. The toilet had crystallized urine stains all over it, and the shower had mildew on the floor and sides. The sink looked like it would soon fall off the wall, razors lined up along the side, and a puddle of soggy soap. That being said, with a top-to-bottom renovation, the place could be cozy.

I didn't want to touch anything, not the flusher, not the sink handles, nothing. If I did touch anything it would be with a piece of toilet paper, which there was none of. One thing was for sure: I wasn't going to much in this bathroom, no matter how bad I needed, not even set my toothbrush down. That would have to wait for work, if it could. I've been living outside, letting dogs that lick their own balls and butts all day also lick my face, but I had some essential boundaries. I definitely had to clean this place before even considering sitting on that toilet seat or using that moldy shower, if I stayed.

Back on the couch my wired eyes kept rolling over and over the place, like I was witnessing some kind of laughable horror. A different side of life it was, not so far outcast from my own, but beyond what I've ever seen. The walls were nicotine yellow. Two wooden small side tables, the finish faded and cigarette burns all along the sides, looked semi-sturdy. The place was one massive ashtray. It's a wonder he hadn't burned the building down. It's a wonder he's alive. But it's no wonder he prefers to be high in the park day and night to avoid this place. It had potential but it was no home, and it was lonely, just like every closet sized dump apartment in this city when you don't have someone to share it with. A guy like him didn't need a home, just a place to finish his runs every here and there without anyone bothering him in the process. I don't doubt this place was illegal, or that the state was paying for it.

Old, brown carpeting — destroyed — covered the floors. More cigarette burns could be found on them, even the sides of the bathroom sink. They seemed to be everywhere, now that I was looking. The TV sat on the floor with a pile of empty forty ounce beer bottles behind it. There was a big, black trash bag that looked like a half-hearted attempt to clean, but never got carried out, brimming with Chinese takeout containers, crusty duck sauce and solidified fried rice stuck to the sides, plus more bottles and cans. Just a counter for a kitchen, a small oven and a sink overflowing with more old, filthy to-go cartons and paper plates, with pizza crusts that looked like petrified wood. The cabinets were dark, seventies paneling that were all crooked, peeling, and half hanging on. I could only imagine what was rotting behind those doors, or was beyond rot at this point.

God knows for how long this trash has been festering, past the point of attracting ants, mice, and roaches. No insect, vermin, or maggot was interested anymore. The place was so small compared to what I had in Brooklyn with Sara. The bathroom had enough space to wash your hands, and put your leg in the shower while sitting on the toilet. But it was close to the park. In that respect, I felt it could be useful for me, if all went well with Tony.

Then, before I knew it, I was half dreaming. The softness of the couch was so soothing that I was out before I knew it. When I woke it was dark. I slept solidly through the entire day. I saw Tony on his bed sleeping face down in his clothes with an unlit cigarette in his hand. His feet were hanging off the bed and he was faintly snoring. It was Saturday night, so I went back to sleep, sitting upright, still in all my clothes. My bones ached, catching up from the other evening and all the other nights where I barely slept, or slept with one eye open, and was up at the crack of dawn.

Tony was gone the next day, and so I left, too. I wasn't sure if I wanted to sleep there again, not because I thought it was so bad, but because it was easier being on my own and I had no way of knowing where he'd be or when he'd be back, or if he really wanted me to stay there for real. We exchanged cell numbers the night before, and I'd wait to hear from him to see if he put the offer out again. He was probably out doing whatever it is he does. I left twenty dollars on his bed, then resolved to do my regular weekend routine in café's, streets, and the park.

Despite all the sleep, I felt nauseous and had a huge headache. Friday night was still working through me. I wanted to head to Brooklyn and see if Sara was working. I needed someone to talk to and connect with, someone to pull me out of this lost feeling. But I don't know if she'd want to see me, if she's even working. Looking like I do, I shouldn't. I'd rather she see me doing well than looking and feeling like this, showing up at her work out of the blue, seeking assurance, especially after all that happened. She would still be resentful, and I couldn't blame her. She knew I didn't think highly of her, and unknowingly looked down on her. As I have, she likely came to realize what an incompetent and insensitive idiot I was in that relationship. But I wouldn't see her. Not soon or ever again. The memory of her would fade more in time, but my remorse never would. I still felt sorry for treating her so carelessly at every turn. If I ever get to be an old man, she'd be chalked up with all the other mistakes. It didn't have to be so, but it was.

A few hours later I found myself sitting on a bench in the park, thinking about Friday and reading a crime book I got from the library. The sun shone on my face and it felt good. It had been so long since we had clear skies. I didn't want to go back to my bench just yet. It was a beautiful spring day, and I remembered what I said to myself about changing. I would try to fulfill that, but for now all I could do was think of how, while waiting for Monday to come, and all the days after.

I tried to avoid going back to Tony's when it got dark, but it was growing cold and I was still fighting for strength. He sent me a text saying he got the money, and thanks, and left the door open if I needed to return. That he wasn't worried to leave the door unlocked said a lot about the place. I can imagine a burglar entering and quickly turning around, running out the way he came in. He didn't know when or if he'd be back tonight, but told me to feel free to go — and pick him up a pack of smokes if I could. So I went back with some food and crashed on the couch, and finished off the book. The next day I left another twenty-dollar bill and the cigarettes Tony requested, in the same spot as before.

Monday morning. I went into work early. 7 a.m. I needed enough time to throw my clothes in the laundry, which smelled like Tony's place. I sat in the dog bath, washing myself with dog shampoo, while my clothes were in the washer. If it wasn't so pathetic I could laugh at the sight of myself. And if Chris and Lee had decided to come in early and discovered me, it would have been sad and disturbing. As always, they came in later. I looked shaven and fresh, clothes damp from taking them out of the dryer early, but clean.

"Good morning, Johny! You're looking chipper today," Lee said, glancing my way with a wink.

"Thought you were growing a beard last week, no? What happened, your girlfriend didn't like it?"

"Nope. Just got the feeling I wanted to shave it all. Got itchy."

He was curious about my personal life, wanted to know if I had a girlfriend. He knows I'm straight, but I think he likes to fish for info to get a better idea of who I am. He wants to know who my friends are, what I'm into, what I do on the weekends, who I'm close to, etc. He's the nosy type and is always asking questions, though the less he knows the better. So far I'd been mostly mum about my life, but at some point it's only fair that he know a little more about me, if he felt he needed that. I just don't know that I have anything presentable to be open about that wouldn't turn him off. What if I opened up and said something that made him peg me as a bad person, then dismissed all the other good things he knew about me as a result? That was what held me back from opening up too soon with anybody.

People started dropping the dogs off; the morning rush. Sometimes the owners dropped them off, but mostly it was their assistants or nannies. It was easy to tell them apart. Chris and Lee were extra friendly and chatty to dog owners - when they came in.

I was by the desk when this girl walked in with Bella. I figured she was probably the new assistant, knowing Bella's owners who usually drop her off. She looked very regular, inexpensive clothes, awkward gait, plainly put together, but cute in a ragamuffin way. She had a jacket covered in animal hair with the buttons falling off; black leggings also covered in hair, and worn looking black boots that came up to her calves. She walked in with a big smile and said hello to Lee right away, not really noticing Chris and me, who were in the back handling the dogs. He was nice to her, introduced himself and asked her if she was Bobby's new assistant; said they had mentioned someone else would be bringing Bella in from now on.

When she spoke she seemed shy, bubbly, shaky voice, always trying to maintain a smile, answering questions with her eyes moving around the room. She wasn't so young – late twenties, maybe early to mid-thirties, but had the oddities of a girl. I walked over to her and stretched my hand out to introduce myself. Her big, brown eyes moved to meet mine. She shook my hand and introduced herself.

Sandra. I thought she'd have a more exotic name, seeing as though she had an ethnic appearance, dark features, olive skin, big almond-shaped eyes. I couldn't tell if she was Mediterranean or Middle Eastern. I noticed why she seemed insecure when I saw her up close: her skin was bumpy with lots of makeup to cover it, heavy on the mascara and eyeliner, too. She was still pretty, but more for her warmth than in a superficial way. There was some tension between us for a second, our eyes locked, and she blushed. I got nervous, for the first time in a while. Even Lee felt it and had a slight smirk as he glanced between our faces before cutting away from us. I broke the stare and squatted to pet Bella, who had already been jumping up and crying for me to acknowledge her.

"Oh, Bella! I missed you, too. Okay, now you get all my attention."

Bella started to lick my face, as she loved to do, while Sandra and Lee were watching. Then she suddenly said, "Nice to meet you. See you later," and abruptly walked out the door without notice or closing the conversation. It was surprising, but we didn't really think twice of it. Lee looked at me and winked, to which I just shook my head. I looked up at him and shook my head, too. He's not the kind of guy I want to know how I feel towards any particular woman. He'd just ruin it by making it really obvious.

Meeting Sandra made me feel a little better throughout the day. I really liked her eyes and that someone like her was now taking care of Bella. I didn't want to get into a relationship with anyone, but I felt like I wanted to know her. I thought of her during the day and waited to see her again when she came to pick up Bella. I felt excited by her, a feeling I hadn't felt in a long time for a woman. I couldn't bring myself to be attracted to any woman in a real way for a while, or even talk to, until today.

When she returned to retrieve Bella, she was blushed and even jumpier than before. It threw me off, but I was still interested. The expectation of what to say to each other stiffened us; it felt rushed. I knew eventually I'd be able to talk to her and make traction in finding out more about her. I just couldn't do it in front of Chris and Lee.

*****

A month later, things had changed for the better. The weather started getting warmer and sleeping in the park became more bearable, when I was out there. I crashed at Tony's all but a few nights except when I had lost the key Tony gave me, and had to wait for him to come back around to make another copy of his set. It had been a couple days or so since I saw Tony last, and I wondered what he'd been up to, hoping he didn't get busted or hurt. I cleaned the apartment of all the trash, bleached all the surfaces, dusted, aired the place out, and it wasn't so bad. It became homey. Being able to use the sinks, showers, and toilet made the place livable. I even bought a new shower curtain and some blankets to cover the couch.

Not so much was happening with Sandra. Seemed we couldn't get past the forced conversation to really talk. She wanted to as much as I did, but it was exasperating to keep trying when we just couldn't connect, and when I could feel her frustration in trying. When she came in she was either dropping off or picking up Bella, and we'd get stuck talking about the same stuff, avoiding eye contact and trying to think up something to say. Sometimes she'd try to ask me questions and, as soon as I got the feeling, I'd change the subject in an attempt to avoid them out of nervousness. Then there'd be a quiet moment and she'd rush out, as she always did, taking it personally. There was no place for a woman in my life anyhow. There was no way I had anything to offer, and no way I had the energy to put up with their emotional ups and downs. Nobody should love me in this state. I was of the mind that it's best not to let anyone close, for their own sake as much as mine.

The girls I'd been with in the past were the types I'd meet while out drinking with friends after work. Some I dated for a while and then we'd rush into living together. Some dates were getting drunk and having sex. Some relationships were one-night stands turned into years of codependence and unhealthy attachments coupled with scarce intimacy. I never really wanted to look into their eyes and admit that they were a stranger, and vice versa. Was there real love? I don't know. There must have been something or it wouldn't have worked, and we wouldn't have kept running back to each other after every fight, feeling it was real love. But I didn't know anything else. This girl Sandra, she would take some time. This would take work. She was skittish and I didn't want to work for something I wasn't sure I even wanted. I also didn't want to follow the same dysfunctional patterns I'd had with my previous relationships, if you can even call them that. I don't believe there is such thing as a perfect relationship, but I just didn't want to play games anymore.

But, I need the companionship of a woman again. I don't care what she looks like, or if she's imperfect, or if nobody else wants her. She can change. I want someone who needs me as much as I need her, and who won't leave me. Sandra seemed like she was just weird enough to be someone who could love me, and who I could love, too. But, I still couldn't decide if I wanted to go forward with her or not.

Sometimes I'd wake to this terror and sadness that my life would never improve, and I will never have someone to share it with, and that I'll never have the security that having money provides. It made me feel hopeless. New York is a bleak place and it's difficult to find people who won't drop you for the next best thing. They're always searching for improvement by association, higher up on the ladder. Many people had treated me as though I weren't good enough in my life. I did the same to Sara, but it wasn't for someone else. It was because I just gave up on everything, including her.

After work I started to develop more of a regime of activities, routes, places I'd stop at, places I'd eat at, places I'd rest at. I began to focus and roam less, started doing Sudoku and crossword puzzles for hours, and even began drawing in an empty sketchbook I picked up at the arts and crafts store. I went to the library and read all kinds of books, classics to modern detective novels, anything I could get my hands on. The boredom wasn't so bad anymore; in fact, it was almost nonexistent. If everything stayed just like this, I could be all right, so long as I didn't want anything more than what I had, and so long as the weather was good.

The only thing that disrupted this schedule was drinking, which threw all my physical and mental energy out the window for a few days. Hanging out with Tony made it hard not to drink, even a little bit, and I'd get hung-over from just a few beers. Booze to him was like blood to a vampire. I never touched drugs since the night I met him, which he never offered because he knew I didn't want any part in it. I had told him straight out a while back that I was all set with that garbage, that I'd been there, done that. His response was a nod of the head and a "Wish it would let me go already, too, man."

I really enjoyed my time with Tony when he was around. He was becoming a true friend and we spent half the week hanging out, the other half he'd be gone in the streets. He talked a lot. I was quiet. He was wild. I was reserved. As different as we were, we had crucial things in common. I was learning a lot from him, didn't know exactly what, but just having a friend like him made everything better. Thinking back to how alone I was before, even with Sara, for such a long time, too. I was sad, and it made me sad to think of it. If anything in my life had improved, it was that I had someone I could talk with about everything, and — even though Tony's crew was a bit gnarly — I was beginning to feel like they were my buddies, too. Paul, Scotty, Jimmy, Hector, Phil, Peter, José, all the guys I met that first night were fixtures by my former go-to park bench. They were there on an almost daily basis, drinking and hanging, getting their drugs, or just swinging by to say hi and talk. The only time they disappeared was when they were in trouble, and most of them had a little dump to go home to, just like Tony, or still lived with their mother. Some of them had girlfriends at home, very patient girlfriends. Not one of them really cared to get clean, or off the streets. They talked about it every once in a while, but it was clear they liked their life, when they had what they needed.

All of them had a story and I think I heard every one of them, because they were all big talkers once they had a few drinks in them. They couldn't wait to tell you where they'd been, what they'd seen, and who they knew, which was nobody I knew. And there were always new tales, brewing from the madness of their daily lives, all completely unpredictable and always criminal.

Most of society looks down on them, but has no idea how appealing these guys really are. Sometimes they're running from the cops, other times they're getting high with them. Sometimes they've got nothing, other times they roll up with money falling out of their pockets, wearing nice clothes for a change, and living in nice hotel rooms. They were careful not to reveal too much of what they were up to, and I didn't want to know. I knew they were all thieves and liars, and that was enough, yet I still trusted them, with everything but my money.

    Sometimes I swung by after work, just to see who was hanging around and talk. They'd be sitting there, watching pretty girls walk by in their spring dresses, catcalling, and acting like they could get some. The girls would ignore them with looks of disgust, but they didn't mind one single bit. It was hard for me to believe there was a sane female out there that would sleep with any of them, but they claimed to get laid on a regular and have multiple girlfriends. I pretended to believe that. They weren't the worst looking guys in the world, not the best, not the richest, not the poorest, in relative terms. Some were worse than others, and those ones didn't even try. The guys were amusing, though. A young girl might find one of them a novelty for a little while before she figured out things weren't going anywhere, ever. The girls wouldn't have to worry about them cheating with other women, just their constant lying, stealing, absentness, and addictions, which was sometimes preferred to infidelity. But there was never a dull moment with these guys, they were fun, and there is nobody quite like any of them. Whenever I stopped by, they treated me well, because they knew I was tight with Tony now.

    All I needed was to be in with Tony and I got respect from most of the street crews who had seen me around with him. People knew him on every block from the park up to Harlem and beyond. When he disappeared for days, he was in every part of the city with every type of person, and the goings on of his life were a mystery to me. I didn't ask, but I listened when he told me what he remembered of it when he'd return, always entertaining stories. Nobody really knew much about me either and they didn't ask anything too personal. Asking too many questions is suspicious. If someone wants to tell you something, they'll tell you. Most I've met around here either talked too much or too little, and didn't believe most of what they heard, unless they saw it.

It was Thursday. I ate lunch in the park until it started raining and I had to run back to work with the remainder of my sandwich. When I returned, Chris was sitting at the desk, wrapping up a phone call. He turned to look at me with a confused expression on his face. When he hung up, he looked down at the phone and then up at me again, under his breath uttering, "Strange, very strange." I had a hunch it had something about me, and instantly my stomach dropped, fearing that perhaps he'd found something out. Again, the suspense that I'd be figured out and kicked to the curb, a feeling that caused me to sabotage so much in my life. I told myself to remain calm and not jump to conclusions, and after he put some papers away he started talking.

"Johny, do you know an elderly woman named Betty?"

"Hmmm…no, that's not ringing any bells. Why?"

"Well, this guy called and asked for you and I said you were on lunch, but then the phone got passed to this old lady and she said she wanted to speak to you. She sounded serious. She left a number and asked if you could call her back at your earliest convenience. I almost thought it was a prank."

"That is strange."

"Here's the number. Might as well call now since you got 15 more minutes 'til lunch is over. Whatever it is."

I went into the grooming room and shut the door for privacy, then just stared at the number for a minute. I hoped it wasn't some bill collector or cop. But, an old lady? That was just puzzling. I didn't want to call, but felt like I had to; I'd already committed by coming in the room, and for sure Chris would ask about it when I walked out. Something inside gnawed at me, hinting that it might be bad news — related to the McDonald's incident, or something to do with my mom...Tony...or Sara...or something else altogether. I couldn't say what. I dialed and, after 10 rings, when I was about to hang up and be done with it, a man answered. I explained that I got a message to call this number. He then confirmed my name.

"Thanks for calling back so soon, Johny. Hold on, I'll get Betty."

Without a reply, he put me on hold. I kept thinking it was some kind of joke, especially when I heard her crackly voice on the other end, sounding like an elderly Katherine Hepburn. Maybe it was Tony playing a joke on me.

"Why, thank you, Johny, for getting back so promptly. We were just about to head out with Jack, but the sooner we talk the better."

I remained silent, mostly because I felt this getting weirder and didn't have the time or energy to talk with some old lady I didn't even know. Under no circumstances did I want to be rude, I just wanted her to get to the point, and fast. She spoke, regularly taking long breaths and pauses in between sentences.

"I know you are at work and probably don't have a whole lot of time to talk on the phone — who does these days? My name is Betty, and my assistant is Harvey, whom you spoke to before."

I stayed silent, so she kept going.

"Here it is: I need someone who can do some in-house dog sitting and walking for my Jack Russell. He is young, needs to play, but doesn't like other dogs. I got your name from one of your clients where you work. Darn, can't remember their name at the moment, but they said you have a way with the dogs there, so I thought I'd reach out. Is this something that might interest you?"

She spoke in a proper manner and was direct. The barrage of information took me a few seconds to process and I muttered "yea" a few times before committing to a real reply.

"I work here full-time, but may be interested in after work or on weekends. I need a bit more information, though."

"Of course, as expected. I hope it's not too much to ask you to come to my home to talk and meet Jack, my dog. I am in a wheelchair and it is difficult for me to get around. I can send a car or have Harvey come get you with my driver, and reimburse you for your time either way. You let me know when is good for you."

She didn't leave space for refusal, which means people probably don't say no to her much. I'm sure she figures I need the money as much as she needs the right person.

"I could do tomorrow evening after my shift. No, no, actually Saturday afternoon is better."

"That works fine. Tell me where I should send the car."

"If you give me your address, it will be easier for me to walk. I have some things to do in the morning and don't know where I'll be. I can make it between 11 and 12."

The offer of a car sounded tempting, but I didn't want to give her Tony's address. I wasn't even sure this was real, although it sounded like it could be. I'd gotten a few offers like this from Uptown Dogs' customers, wanting me to walk their dogs on the weekends, or in-house dog sitting while they were away, but I was afraid I'd be too unreliable and passed. Betty gave me her address and I told her to expect me Saturday at noon. She was cordial and appreciative and said, "thank you" three times, although I almost wanted to call back and cancel. The thought of committing to more work could be something I could regret, but I figured I'd give it a chance. Something in me wanted to meet this woman, based on the way she spoke and the mystery surrounding who she might be. I couldn't pinpoint it exactly, but I felt compelled to follow through and be punctual.

Later that night I saw Tony in the park. I stopped by to see who was hanging out. I needed to be social, to pass the time and get out of my head. It had been five days since I saw him and he looked horrible. I don't think he got much sleep in these days and I became nervous just to make contact with him. He gave me a back pat that I retracted from, he reeked of booze, and looked wrecked from whatever drugs he'd been taking. It wasn't the same Tony I knew. His eyes looked like raccoon eyes, surrounded by deep, dark circles, and hollow cheeks. I'd only seen him sober on occasion, mornings mostly, but he looked like an stranger to me now. This must be the bottom he cycles up from, one I've never seen before until now.

"What's up Johny? Haven't been around for a minute, but was thinking of you."

"I was thinking of you, too. How you doing? You been around the house?"

"No, no. Got tied up with some stuff the past few days and I'm staying with a friend in the Bronx to help them out with something. Definitely, later. I need some sleep soon."

"Yeah, you look a little spent, take care of yourself. I gotta run and do some things. I'll be there in a few hours, if you wanna get a pizza, let me know and I'll pick one up."

"Cool. Thanks." He smiled and was about to say more. I'm probably the only person he knows that talks about getting pizza and not booze and drugs.

I wouldn't see him later. He doesn't care about food.

I started walking away until I felt his hand on my shoulder. Then, his serious voice, the one where he's about to ask for something, again. I knew it was coming.

Now, Tony had already gotten a lot from me. I'd regularly bought him beers, coffee, smokes, and food, and he never returned the favor, though he always said he'd get me back, which I knew he wouldn't. He'd come to me and ask for a week of rent in advance, sometimes two weeks, and in that time he'd always come and ask for more. It was no big deal, but I didn't want to fund his drug habit and I was tired. It never ended. What if something happened and I had to leave his place after paying him all this time in advance? Living there was still a good deal and I was thankful, but there wasn't much security to what would happen month to month, or day to day. Reliable shelter costs money in the form of leases, security deposits, first and last months' rent, background checks, etc. I just hoped he didn't get busted and I didn't get booted suddenly as a result. I still didn't have enough money to get my own place, nor did I want to spend all that money I had worked so hard to save. I'd have to live in a boarding house in the ghetto, and that comes with its own, worse, problems. I don't think I'd ever afford my own place this close to work and the park, and I got paid under the table, so had no income to speak of on paper. If it weren't for his apartment I'd be back on the bench, so my best option was to take the bad with the good.

"Think you can spot me a little something? Got to pay someone off tonight and they ain't kidding around. After that I just want to go home and get to bed. I get my check in a few days, so I can pay you back, or just take it off the rent."

Oh yeah, his disability check. Somehow he scammed the state into thinking he is injured enough to get monthly funding for his lifestyle. Years ago he fell off a ladder at a worksite, milked it as far as he could to now be seen as an invalid, at least that's what he said. By the time he got his check he owed everyone money, and none of us ever saw it again, maybe just the drug dealers and only because he had to pay his debts to buy more drugs. I thought I had a few dollar bills in my pocket and was going to pull it out to show him that's all I had, but when I did it was more than a few dollars. Wrong pocket. There were a few twenty-dollar bills in my hand and I'd already started saying that I really didn't have enough to help him out until I looked down. Without even asking, he reached in my hand and grabbed it. Walking backwards, he let out a dramatic "thank you" with his hands in prayer position pointed towards me before turning around to swagger off into the night. I watched him for a second, his silhouette. His clothes were baggy from losing weight, and under the street lamps his hair looked extra greasy. He took a long drag from his cigarette and let it out into the air in a trail of victory and defeat. I was reminded of a comic book character, one fighting between extremes of strength and weakness. But I still admired him for being untouchable.

Of course I knew he wouldn't come home later, and of course he didn't. He strolled in a few days after just as the morning sun shone through the dirty windows. I woke for a moment to see him go into his room and fall onto his bed like he'd just escaped from the trenches. He'd sleep for days, and I wondered how long he could keep going like this.

No matter how many times I had beat myself up for feeling like a failure, I had nothing to complain about, and neither did he. We weren't stressed out like most people, working round the clock, up to our ears in commitments and bills, with screaming kids and bitter wives at home, losing ourselves in the game of it all and trying to survive our own delusions, reaching for anything to keep us afloat. No, we had our own problems, but we are free minded. We found a way to live and think off the radar. We don't care about the rules. We are men. Nobody controls us and we don't give in to the lies around us. It's always a trade-off.

When I arrived at Betty's the next day, I stood before a beautiful townhouse facing the park. Never in my life had I been inside a residence like this. I didn't know how to approach, if it was even the right place, but I walked up the staircase leading to the door, rang the bell and waited, looking and feeling out of place. I was earlier than expected and hoped she'd be there.

A tall man in a black dress shirt and gray slacks opened the door after a few rings. He had a slight British accent and blue eyes, with clean-cut dirty blonde hair.

"Johny, eh?" he said reaching his hand out to shake mine, with one side of his mouth raised.

"Nice to meet you." I shook his hand.

He had a good grip, which made me strengthen mine.

"Harvey. We spoke for a moment on the phone yesterday. Please come in. Glad you could make it."

He wasn't the pretentious type at all. I couldn't make out how to otherwise judge him. He was older than me, by five to ten years, courteous, but more of a regular guy than an elite type, despite his expensive looking clothes. The accent, Irish or Scottish, couldn't tell. I never knew what to expect from people behind the doors of these places. I wasn't sure if he was an assistant, family member, or caretaker.

When I entered, Harvey gestured to some big, soft chairs in the adjacent room. He then turned to me and said that he'd be back, that Betty was not quite ready yet, that she had a difficult morning and needed a little more time. It was no problem and I said so. He thanked me for my patience before scaling the winding staircase in the entrance hall.

Once out of sight, it was safe to express my awe at this place. I had tried to act unfazed when entering, not really looking around, but now I was free to be humbled by it. It was something straight out of a fairy tale — elegance, wealth, and beauty. I'd always claimed I didn't care to be rich, but to witness how they live made me feel nothing short of envy and insignificance. To own a property like this, to walk in every day and make myself at home, was beyond my comprehension. But I could only feel out of place in this setting, like I should keep quiet and not touch anything or I'd be humiliated, like a peasant, and my adoration would expose me as less-than. As beautiful as it all was, this kind of wealth was uncomfortable, and that's how I felt sitting there. Just beyond these walls is a city, a world, where so many have nothing.

I got up from the chair to observe the art that hung on the walls. In the entrance hall hung a sizeable crystal chandelier and a dome ceiling that went up a few floors. Everything was white and gold, along with the tile floor, all with intricate carvings. Gorgeous plush rugs were carefully laid out, full of vibrancy, color, and details.

Much of the art collection comprised landscape paintings. The waiting room where I sat was cozier, with lush peaches and yellows. The art was of a different tone there than in the hall. Some were abstract, Picasso-looking type stuff. Other works were random, photographs of the city and other exotic places. There were countless portraits of women, their faces and bodies. The art taken together was eclectic, but fit together nicely, as if someone with exquisite taste had curated everything. Betty, perhaps.

And then there was this one photograph, right in the middle of all the paintings in the center of the wall that grabbed me. I couldn't find any way to describe it to myself or identify what magnetism I felt towards it. It was a woman's face against a backdrop of the city, sitting atop a tall building on the roof. She may have been nude, as the photo revealed her shoulders and cut just above her breasts. Her hair fell flat on both sides of her face and she stared straight ahead at the camera bearing a vulnerable countenance and leaning forward. No smile. Her eyes were big and young, and her hair reflected rich sunlight. The contrast in the photo accentuated the freckles all over her face and chest. I approached it to get a better look, feeling as though it kept drawing me in.

"That one's my favorite, too. There's a story behind that picture. Remind me to tell you about it on the way out."

Her words came so suddenly that I jumped. Recognizing it was Betty, I prepared myself to turn around and make a formal introduction. My palms started sweating and I hoped my voice wouldn't break, but I managed to speak.

"Hi. Pleasure to meet you."

Betty smiled, looking up at me from her wheelchair as I approached. I felt like I should take her hand, but refrained. I wondered if that were she in the picture; it was hard to tell because she had aged so much. But then I saw her freckles, the same as in the photo. They brightened her face and gave her the innocent look of a teenager.

"Also a pleasure, Johny. Thank you for arriving on time. I'm sorry I made you wait."

There was a silent moment, then Harvey entered from a side door as quietly as she had. He looked at Betty and then at me, then sat on the armrest of the sofa between us.

"Shall we?" He asked looking at Betty.

"Sounds good. Come, Johny, let's meet Jack in the study."

The three of us went to the elevator around the corner, Betty steering herself in her motorized chair. We were silent the whole time and looked ahead at the doors as we rode to the fifth floor. The elevator had mahogany walls and a mirror in the back, which I pressed up against in order to make room.

"How's it looking out there today, Johny? Did the sun come out?" Harvey asked, glancing back at me for a moment.

"It's beautiful. The sun is out. Looks like it's gonna be a nice afternoon."

"We deserve it. After the harsh winter we just had. Jack will certainly enjoy running in the grass again," Betty added.

The elevator doors opened and a large, beautiful room revealed itself. There were more paintings, more ornate rugs, big couches, and chairs, with a grand wooden desk at the opposite end facing us. Everything was dark, blue, gray, green, earthy browns and reds. Behind the desk was a floor-to-ceiling window spanning the width of the room. A majestic, unobstructed view of the park spread out before us, and the buildings that neatly line it. Despite the fact that we weren't high up, by New York City standards, it was still a classic view; the quiet wall of towers that faced the trees, in a park where I once slept.

From behind the couch emerged Betty's beloved Jack Russell, with his head down, wagging his tail and looking timidly at me. He was small and seemed like he could still be a puppy, though his eyes were older. His ears were back and he wouldn't come fully out into the room. He kept his safe distance, stretching his front paws ahead of him and whimpering while looking at Betty and Harvey.

"Johny, please sit. Jack is a bit shy with newcomers, but he will warm up to you."

I sat on the sofa against the sidewall. Betty motioned Jack to her chair from behind her desk in front of the window, then scooped him onto her lap and zoomed over in my direction. He was scared as she placed him near me on the floor, but he overcame his fear to sniff all the tempting odors of other dogs on my jeans. I started to pet him, and as I did he looked up, his tail wagging faster. He was really cute, small for an adult dog, and I too felt bad that he was cooped up in this house alone with them. Animals don't care how fancy their home is, or how rich or poor the people who have them are. They just want to play and be loved.

I felt like he needed me, and I was positive whatever Betty had to offer would appeal to me, too. Both she and Harvey were watching my every move in a subtle way.

"They did say you have a way with dogs," Betty said.

I didn't ask who referred me, but I wondered and wanted to know. I'd ask another time.

"He's a great dog, very sweet," I replied.

"So here's the deal, Johny. Neither Harvey nor I can give energetic Jack the care he needs. He needs to run and play and be outside, as well as inside. I am old and everything is so much effort for me. I can't walk in the park like I used to, and if Jack got off the leash or if there was a problem with another dog, it would be impossible for me to help him. Harvey is also busy assisting me in household and business affairs. He's been walking Jack for a while now, but sometimes he has to rush back here to help me with something. Plus, Harvey is meant to be here with me. He is not a dog walker. My health is compromised and I have rough days where I need to be on oxygen and see the doctor. It's not fair that Jack spends so much time alone like this. I feel horrible about it. I'd like to get another dog for him, but I can't handle that. We've had a few dog sitters and walkers here and there, but many of them were young and unreliable, and moved on to other careers and places. I can understand that. I tried bringing him to Uptown Dogs a while back, but the other dogs bullied him and I could tell he was unhappy there. I know you have a busy schedule already, but even if just a few days a week, whenever you can, would be a great help. It's been hard to find the right person who seems mature enough to trust and take this seriously. Take as much time as you need to decide if this is feasible."

As she spoke, I watched her with intensity. She had this way. I picked it up on the phone conversation with her as well. It was her articulation, eye contact, and absence of eye contact, of creating expression, persuasion, and passion. Her blue eyes sparkled and, when she turned to look out the big window, the light coming in made her skin look doll white. And she almost made it impossible for me to say no. Not because she was manipulative, but because she inspired some understanding inside me. I might have agreed to anything she asked.

She turned back to me and I glimpsed the beautiful woman in the photograph downstairs. After a few seconds I finally moved my eyes from her, breaking the moment they locked. She was reading my reaction and waiting some kind of answer, despite her having told me to take my time deciding. Without realizing, I looked out the window.

I felt good around her, in her house. Then I reached down to put Jack on my lap. I don't know why, because I never pick up dogs and place them on my lap, not even the small ones. Usually I got down to their level. But in a way I was already following Betty's actions, and Jack seemed receptive. He kept trying to lick my face, same as Bella loves to, and I started laughing as he climbed on my chest and started to play. He was gentle and smelled like a puppy. His mouth was half open and he was going for my belt buckle as he half-heartedly bit it and tried to and engage me. I wanted her to wait for my reply and watch me as I watched her.

Looking into Jack's eyes, I said, "I think we can work something out."

After I said this I turned to Betty and she smiled at me. I smiled back and continued to play with Jack, letting him nibble my hands and paw my face.

"I have time on the weekends and can come after work a few days during the week. How much time do you need me for?"

"Well, an hour to two on the weekdays would be ideal. Enough time for a solid walk and to play with him here, keep him amused for a bit. He doesn't get much other activity. On the weekends, I don't know how busy you are, but two walks a day would be great. You could stay here between walks for a few hours, if you want, and lounge around the house and eat with us, or come and go as needed. It's hard to tire him, given he's a young Jack Russell. He has an unbelievable amount of energy. I've had to replace a few chairs and couches and other items due to his biting and chewing."

I started to say something, but she began speaking again.

"I know. It sounds more like a babysitting situation, but instead of a child, this is a dog. Jack is my baby. He means a lot to me and it pains me that he doesn't get the attention he needs. If it doesn't work for either of us at some point, then just give me some notice and I will do the same. But so long as you are an honest person and can take this seriously, and are good to Jack, there is no reason why it shouldn't work. I think so far you seem like a good fit and Jack likes you. I trust his judgment."

Betty may sound like an eccentric to many, and at one time I might have thought her one. But I realized as she spoke that she seemed desperate. Jack must be all she has. Maybe she has kids, maybe she doesn't, maybe she's a divorcée, a widow, or her husband is hiding somewhere in this huge house. Maybe she has family, grandkids, friends, etc. — or maybe not. One thing is for sure, though: she loves Jack. My guess is that she's profoundly lonely. I know that feeling more than I'd like to admit.

"Johny, I can pay you well."

She spoke this with intention after a long moment of silence. That got my attention, as she knew it would, and I turned my head from Jack to her and looked into her eyes. I felt she wanted me to know how much all this meant to her, so that I could give her as much as I could.

"We could do hourly or salary, whatever you prefer. Fifty dollars an hour to start. If you can commit to a schedule, we can do a salary of twenty hours a week. All you need to do is show up regularly and take care of Jack. The more time you can spend with him, the better."

This was pretty good.

"No taxes?" I asked.

"We can do either way, whatever you prefer."

"I prefer no taxes."

"Can you start today?"

"Yes."

"Great. Harvey, please show Johny where we keep Jack's leash and toys and bring them into the park. Show him the places Jack likes and where you can let him run off-leash. I need to rest."

She looked content to have gotten her way, as I'm sure she always does. She also looked relieved that her guilt over Jack's situation could be remedied. Her face turned gray for a moment and she seemed rushed to go. She motored over to me, grabbed my hand with both of hers and looked into my eyes. "Thank you, thank you, thank you ever so much, Johny. I have a good feeling about this."

She then cupped her hand around Jack's ears, who was now sitting on the floor beside me, and started baby talking to him. I never met anyone who said thank you as often as her.

"My little baby is finally going to have some fun."

Then she wheeled herself out of the room, leaving Harvey and me to take Jack into the park. The dog ran circles around us the entire time, with his tongue hanging out of his mouth and his ears flopping. Sheer happiness. Betty was right. This dog had so much life. He never stopped running.

*****

In over half a year, since January, my life took so many turns. It was unexpected, random, and by summer I felt many of my problems were behind me. Summer had that effect on us all. The issues that lingered were too small for me to worry about anymore, or at least they were out of the way for the time being. I didn't want to feel like I had last winter — stuck, angry, and hopeless, nothing to look forward to. The fact that I was making money and keeping busy gave me the esteem I'd been missing for so long.

I never told Tony about Betty. If he knew I was working for someone like her, he'd try to exploit me by raising rent or asking questions. Chris and Lee knew, but very little. I gave no details. They seemed to have their own problems to juggle, and were barely around each other for a while. Only one came to work at a time and, when the other came in, they'd part company without uttering a word. It put me in a shaky position, but I said nothing, and was glad that I wasn't involved with them personally to get dragged in the middle.

"Ol' lady's got you working hard on the weekends, huh? You never told me how that's going — how is it? What's she like? Where in the city does she live?"

I started smirking because I didn't want to give Lee too much info. I was sure he'd been wondering for some time about it and waited for the right moment to ask.

"I'm working there on the weekdays and the weekends, but it's not so bad. Nice dog. She's alright. It's only been a few weeks but I really like it."

Lee was nodding his head and repeated "great" a few times as he searched my face for something more. He then returned to the paperwork he was busy with. He had a question, but wouldn't come out with it right away, so I kept going. I knew he was wondering how this woman found out about me, what kind of situation I have with her, who she is, how much she pays me, and I didn't have the answers to all these questions. If I did, I still wouldn't tell him. He would want me to try to sell her something or produce something for him out of it; feeling like the opportunity should be credited to him.

"I can't complain."

I wanted to say something else but couldn't, so I just repeated myself.

"Nope, can't complain."

My lack of real response was no shock to Lee. It was typical, and he went back to work.

"Good, glad it worked out. You should have her stop by sometime. I'd love to meet this little Jack Russell, too."

He got up to head out and, as Sandra was coming in, he held the door open for her, then turned and gave me a sly look. It was rare that Sandra came into the shop when I was alone, and it was only because Lee was actually getting his own coffee today. He wanted to be there less and less lately and took advantage of any distraction he could to leave. I had been there long enough that both he and Chris trusted me to do what needed to be done. They were out enjoying the nice weather, or dealing with whatever they were dealing with.

Sandra and I were caught off guard. We had to try to make some conversation of this tension, and it was quiet at first. We watched Bella to avoid eye contact, and talked about the weather. Then she surprised me.

"So, do you want to hang out sometime?"

I hesitated. We were both looking down at Bella when she asked this and, without looking up, I knew her face was flushed, as was mine. I wanted to say yes, but I started getting scared and wasn't even sure the words could make it out of my mouth. What if things didn't go well? What if she likes me too much? What if, by saying yes, I am suddenly held to some standard or commitment? In spite of all my fleeting fears I said, "Sure. How about a movie?"

She looked surprised that I accepted. I don't know why I suggested a movie, but it just came out. It seemed appropriate and casual, and I felt I should be the one to make the plan. I had hoped and dreaded for this moment to come. Here it was. A real date. Tomorrow night. In spite of feeling imperfect, I was ready to get out there and try to date again.

"Okay. I'll find out what's playing and let you know tomorrow after work."

"Sounds good. Yea, sounds good. See you tomorrow." I replied.

The whole thing felt forced, because I was inexperienced in dating. It was a lot of pressure just to think about and we were both painfully nervous.

I hoped it didn't change things for the worse. I hoped I wouldn't fall too hard for her or, worse, vice versa. I hoped it wouldn't make things strange at work. I hoped she wouldn't be one of those needy girls looking for someone to take care of them. I hoped she didn't want to get into a relationship too fast. I also hoped she would never find out about my real life, where I lived, that I was homeless, that I was a jerk, etc. I could handle none of that. I wanted to be on a fresh slate and take it slow.

When Lee came back he was ready to comment, as usual.

"Sandra was smiling walking down the street. What happened? Did you finally ask her out?"

"Nope, she asked me, believe it or not. There was a quiet moment when you walked out the door and we were just standing there. She caught me by surprise. We're gonna catch a movie tomorrow after work."

"Really? She's more aggressive than I'd have pegged her for, but yes, I can see that. She's really into you, Johny. We all knew, plain as day. She stares at you every time she walks in. Are you excited?"

There were a few moments of silence.

"Of course I'm excited. She's adorable. I had a feeling she'd ask me out one of these days," I joked.

"Its cause you're a good-looking guy. If I wasn't married and you weren't straight, just saying." He winked back at me while walking to the grooming room. Sometimes it grossed me out when he acted all flirty like that. I bet he cheated on Chris.

It dawned on me that I wanted to ask Sandra about Betty, if she was the one who referred me, and if she knew Betty and how. Tomorrow night I would ask. I couldn't think of who else might have put in a good word. I had thought of her immediately when Betty stated that someone said I had a way with the dogs.

That night Tony was sitting on the couch nodding off a four-day bender. The place was starting to feel like my own apartment and seeing him back reminded me it wasn't.

When he woke I told him about Sandra and his reaction was encouraging.

"Yes! Finally! You need a decent girl in your life. I was getting worried that you might be a little hotel-motel, like those guys you work for."

"Yeah, well, you would love that. Then you'd try to get with me and take all my money."

"Hey, relax, you," Tony replied laughing, looking shocked by my sarcastic words.

"I see those girls you hang out with. You don't really fool around with them, do ya? Better get checked out is all I can say."

"Don't be pointing your finger when you ain't even getting any. Besides, those girls would bend over backwards for me if I asked. They're nice girls with good hearts, so don't judge. If they're cool with getting what I got, I'm cool with getting what they got," he replied with some sass.

We laughed. It was all a joke. I doubted he could get it up, but knew he liked to give the appearance he still had the swing. No doubt he was just using them to buy him booze and drugs. That was his only real use for women that I could see.

"No, really, pal, I'm happy for you. Hope it goes well. Are you nervous?"

"Yea. I'm really nervous. I'm sweating just thinking about it."

He reached in his pocket and pulled out a bunch of pills. They landed all over the couch, all different ones, and he started to pick them up and pull out the couch cushions until he was sure he got them all.

"Here, this will take the edge off," he said as he passed me a pink oval pill. Take it tomorrow a half hour before you guys meet up."

I pocketed it, because I knew it would help, whatever it was, even though I knew I'd regret taking it. But then I reached in my pocket and swallowed it out of compulsion. He saw and said nothing. I didn't really know why, but I already felt anxious for tomorrow and wanted to let loose right now. It had been so long since I'd been out on a date, and so long since I was with a woman besides Sara. The thought of it made my heart race and stomach clamp up.

Tony was a pharmacist, a chemist, and a doctor when it came to drugs, legal or not. He seemed to know about every pill out there, so long as it was a controlled substance. I had a weakness for things when they were freely offered. I was never a druggie in my life but tried some of them out when I was younger and was always eager to experiment with my friends, nothing hard though. Something in me said to just take it; it was free. But it never really was free, as cliché as that sounded. It always just fucked up my life more than it already was and led to depression for a few days afterwards, just like alcohol. I'm past the age where that stuff runs through me in a day. Instead it brings personal drama to the surface, and the feeling that I don't know what's true anymore. Being sober is more numbing than being high.

"Wanna get a drink?" Tony asked.

"Sure, why not."

"Bring it in the park or hit the bar?"

"Let's go cheap and brown bag it. Easy on the wallet."

We walked to the bar around the corner because Tony was looking for some kid that owed him sixty bucks. Couldn't find him. It was surprising that someone owed him money rather than the other way around, and he couldn't believe this kid ripped him off. Sometimes the cons get conned with their own game by an amateur. I was afraid he would try to ask me for more money again, but he knew not to push it, and somehow he had money and paid for mine for a change. No doubt he stole something, sold something, robbed someone. As we stood at the entrance looking into the bar, some of the guys inside saw Tony and signaled for him to come in.

"It's on me, come on in," they shouted when they saw his head peek in the door.

"Do you mind? They'll probably buy you one, too," Tony asked as he turned to me, already stepping in.

"Course not."

They bought us both drinks, these two guys in their fifties who looked like they sat on these barstools everyday from opening to close. Their faces and noses were beet red, big bellies hanging over their jeans. Both probably the type who just want to talk your ear off all night in exchange for picking up your tab. I'm sure that's why they love Tony. I've seen him sit through that just to get drunk or high on someone else's dollar. It's the only time I've ever seen him quiet.

The two of us, Tony and I, made an odd couple. You'd suspect we met on unlikely terms, like any mismatched pair. There were always those twosomes in the streets that looked like polar opposites, but united over some unconventional circumstance. Sometimes you take what's in front of you, then by coincidence you get along and survive together.

Our circles are never the winners' circles; we'll go with anyone because we have little pretentions. And these duos make the best friendships because nothing is held back and there are no games. That's Tony and me. We look different. We think different. We're from different backgrounds. It didn't matter.

I am unskilled labor and Tony is unemployable. We have no formal education to speak of and no reputable experiences, references, successes, or social graces. We are the perfect modern tragedy. That's the basis of how guys like us join on the streets, usually due to drugs, alcohol, crime, homelessness, desperation of some sorts, or accident, to follow some path of quid pro quo together. If you're still slightly sane living on the streets, you pair up with people to make it easier. If you're crazy, then most likely you're a loner. That seemed to be the rule of thumb.

Tony talked with these guys for the next ten minutes as we drank the beers they bought us. I could tell he was waiting to see if they'd offer to buy him another, but they didn't, so he motioned for us to leave and told the guys he'd buy them a round tomorrow. I'm sure they knew better than to believe that. People were always buying him drinks and drugs and giving him money, just because he was cool. He had a way with everybody. It was hard to believe he was a supposed kingpin at one time, but all the other guys vouched that it was true. These days, he settled to low level, low risk, thievery to get by. He was always trying to hustle someone or sell some junk, which somehow sold eventually, always such random things. I once saw him sell a plastic bag full of used clothing, swimming shorts, button ups and jeans, probably stolen from a gym locker he broke into. He walked into a bar and sold everything to his drunken friends, and for more than they'd be worth if they were new. I'll never forget watching him from outside present the clothes and talk these guys into buying them, and the looks on their faces as they reached into their wallets and handed over the money. Sometimes I think people just wanted to give him money because they knew he wanted it so badly, like it was bread for a starving person.

In the liquor store I got a pint of vodka and Tony got rum. On the way out, a group of guys saw him and all started shaking his hand and patting his back, guys full of tattoos and missing teeth, all speaking Spanish. He talked to everyone, but I got sick of waiting and he took the hint. When he caught up to me he explained, "Old buddies from the joint." I laughed at how funny his life was. It was impossible to walk anywhere with him without getting stopped. No wonder he loved the streets. He had everything he wanted.

We found a bench and sat, drinking from our brown bags. I didn't listen to him talk because the pink pill had kicked in and I was too deep in my own thoughts to focus. It was speed. All I could think about was Sandra. The more I thought about her, the more I feared it was a bad idea to get involved. There were so many variables, all stacked up against the odds that maybe, just maybe, things could actually work. I craved to have someone close that I was willing to chance it all. I desired her and, whatever the repercussions, it was worth a try.

The drunker I got the more I started to forget and the more I started to talk about myself. I never loosened up like this, and everything rolled out in hyper succession. Tony started asking me questions. Questions about my family, where I grew up, what sort of stuff I was into, when and why I moved to NYC. I didn't even know the answers to any of these questions myself. We had gotten into some personal chatting before, but not much. Most of all, I told him about my mother and he completely understood, nodding constantly when I talked of her. I hadn't seen or spoken to her in so long and felt horrible about it. If I called her tomorrow she wouldn't mention the fact I had neglected to keep in touch. She was always so agreeable and accepting, too much so, to the point where she never addressed issues or spoke her mind, but rather kept it all in and pretended she didn't notice. Part of me wanted her to be upset at me, so that I would be pushed to keep in contact; I didn't want her to put up with my crap, but if she nagged me I might not want to keep in touch, either. She was better than putting up with that. And I don't know why I just didn't dial her number and get it over with instead of feeling down about it all the time.

On the other hand, Tony was a mama's boy. He talked to his mother in Puerto Rico every day and, while I never understood their conversations, I could tell he was still her baby. He would never grow up and would most likely return to Puerto Rico someday to care for her, while blowing all his money on booze down there. She'd take care of him. He kept saying that he was going to plan a trip to see her real soon, but he'd been saying that for months already and I doubt it would happen anytime in the near future. A few times he said I should go with him, and that — if I did — I'd likely never want to come back to this city ever again. I wonder if she knows, or has any idea, how fucked up he is all the time. Knowing his past she probably does, and has accepted him anyway.

"My mom has a beautiful house. It's nothing big, but there's lots of land and the beach ain't too far. She's got this garden with all these vegetables growing, too. People stop by to help her cause they know how hard she works with the animals and the upkeep of the place, and she doesn't have much money. Woman is 65 years old and strong as an ox. I should be down there with her. I feel so bad about leaving her all alone. Next time I go, you're coming with me, Johny. We can start over down there."

"I'd love to. I really hope I get to meet her someday. When was the last time you were there?"

"Too long. Way too long. Almost six years. I used to go down twice a year, but after I got out of the joint, I didn't have the money and energy like I had before."

"Wait until you see it. It's a paradise; coconuts growing on the trees, green jungles, beautiful beaches, beautiful women, always sunny. My mom would let us stay as long as we wanted. I wouldn't offer this invitation to just anyone. I trust you, and I know you need to get out of here as much as I do."

"Let's start planning for it, Tony. I'll start saving and you do the same. I don't ever wanna come back to this place. I was thinking about it the other day, I'm done here. I'm not happy. I'm so tired of feeling like I'll never make it, or have enough to live, or be good enough for everyone's stupid standards here. I'm so tired of it."

I was flattered by the offer, but wasn't sure if he was for real. I'd go with him if I could, if it actually happened. Something told me he'd never get clean enough to detach from this place.

Before I knew it my bottle was empty and I wanted more, but Tony was yawning. I guess this was his day off, for a change. The only problem now was what to do all night and how to get to sleep. I just hope I can make it to work tomorrow and be good enough for the date with Sandra. It figures that the day I need my rest the most is the day I won't have it. I was now feeling the effect of the pill full blast. My jaw was grinding. If only Tony didn't give it to me. I don't like this feeling because I know it's followed by a crash. I'm too old to be doing this stuff.

"I can't do it with ya, pal. I'm spent."

"Do what?" I asked.

"You're all hopped up, and I wanna party with ya, but I'm demolished. This week I went on a mad run. Thought you were gonna take that thing tomorrow, anyway."

"Why'd you give me an upper? Figured it would be a downer so I'd be relaxed on the date."

"Yeah, I didn't realize it until I saw you take it, meant to give you the downer so you'd be cool. Sorry, man. At least you didn't take it with her. She'd have probably thought you were a weirdo."

"Well, that makes me feel better. Thanks." I replied sarcastically.

"Stop, it was an honest mistake. My eyes are getting bad. I really do need to rest, feel like absolute shit today, don't know why."

That he didn't know why he felt lousy escaped me. His body is so used to abuse, but eventually it all catches up.

The thought of being left alone tonight was an immediate downer in itself. I wanted to hang out and move around and he was ready to go home and go to bed. My heart beat out of my chest. He took another pink pill from his pocket and put it in front of his face, looking at me.

"You'd really like it if I took this right now, wouldn't you?"

He laughed, looked at me, looked at the pill, threw it in his mouth and dry swallowed it. I'm sure he needed a lot more than one to feel anything, but it was a start.

"Sleep is for the dead. And there's more of those, so don't worry about that. I even got a bunch of downers for landing gear."

"I feel like moving."

"Let's get some more drinks," he said, getting up and motioning for me to join.

When I got up to walk, I felt the Vodka go right to my head. Tony, after drinking twice as much as me, looked like he always looked. He was such a pro that I wondered how much booze and drugs it took for him to feel anything. His body was a human trash receptacle, and it actually baffled me he was still alive some days. There were a few times I woke and saw him crashed on his bed, in all his clothes, looking dead. I was relieved to check his wrist to see his heart was still beating.

"Do me a favor, man," I started. "I just don't wanna hang with any of your freaky cracker jack friends tonight. I like those guys, but some of them are bugs."

"What? Which freaky friends you talking about?"

I suddenly felt like I might have crossed a line, but then he shot me a wry smile. He knew the guys I was referring to, and I'm pretty sure he felt the same way about them most days. The other night he was hanging with some southern straggler in cowboy clothes. He smelled like he hadn't taken a shower for a week. I don't know if Tony knew or cared, but I noticed and couldn't stand ten feet from the guy without covering my nose. I figured he probably bought Tony booze so Tony tolerated him as long as seemed necessary. No doubt he robbed the guy, or ripped him off in some way. Tony is a master of the game where he takes other peoples' money to fetch them drugs or something illegal, and never returns. Later they see him and he always has some elaborate story, a reverse guilt trip, where they forgive him and say sorry for overreacting. Sometimes they give him their money a second time to get ripped off again. They know in their gut he was probably lying, but he made people feel so bad for doubting his lies that they gave in time and time again. Part of his scam was that he was nice to everyone's face and always got back to people. He always had an excuse that he defended endlessly and it would cover just about anything he did, and there was nothing you could counter it with. The smart ones don't give him anything in the first place, everyone else kept hoping they'd get him to follow through eventually, because they had no other connections.

"No problem. I don't like half of them either. Damn freaks is right. Half of them owe me money, and the other half I owe money. I really want to start stepping back from that whole crew. Some of them don't even brush their teeth. That's one thing that really gets me sick. I never went a day in my life without brushing twice and flossing, and that's why I got nice teeth to show for it. Have you ever smelled Larry's breath? Smells like he brushes his teeth with a tuna fish."

He was right about that. Tony had great teeth. It was the only thing he was regular with. I'd seen him carry his portable toothbrush in his pocket and even take it out in public to dry brush his teeth after he smoked. We have that in common, we both keep up with ourselves and wear clean clothing. Looking at all the filthy guys in the park and on the streets only made me become more vigilant about keeping myself in shape.

We headed back to the bodega, drunk at that point. We were laughing and talking loud, walking in the streets between cabs, up to no good, imitating and making fun of people we knew from the park. It felt like we were teenagers again. I hadn't laughed that hard for a long time. I looked around at the city lights for a second. After all these years here, I still have moments of wonder looking at this place. Other times, most times, I want to get out like my sanity depends on it.

We both had a few bucks, so we started bar hopping, buying only the cheapest beers and flirting with cute girls, which I was better at than Tony. He was too thirsty and had this macho Latino thing that scared them away. Every time things were going good for me with a girl, he would come along and be overly aggressive and ruin it. It also could have been because he looks like a criminal, which was my first impression when I saw him. The girls probably thought we were a package deal, and it was clear they didn't want him around getting so close to them. It was annoying. I started looking at Tony, he was acting like an ass and I was embarrassed at having him for company. That might be cool in the streets with his chics, but in a bar it wasn't. And then I noticed something. Tony had sneakily picked a girl's wallet out of her jacket, which hung on the backside of the chair. I saw him turn for a few seconds, loot it, then slide it back in the pocket. When he was done, he reentered the conversation, looking confident, took a deep breath then started back up with his flirting routine until she walked away. I sat back and watched him for the next ten minutes repeat this process.

There was another girl by the bar with her purse near her. She looked wasted, but took his hand as he playfully led her to the dance floor. He held her purse without her seeing then left her dancing as she joined a circle of girls she knew. Laughing while walking backwards and still facing them, Tony retreated to the corner trying to look casual, removed the money and cell phone from the purse, then returned it to the table in a mid-dance move back to the floor with the circle of girls. Nobody saw but me, and I couldn't help to think it was like watching a movie, but so much better. I saw him eye a few more while scanning the room for anyone who might be watching. The last target was a bag hanging from the back of a chair. He headed to the bathroom immediately after grabbing it. When he came out he threw something to the floor and gave me an urgent look that he was heading out. I looked around to make sure nobody saw, and they didn't, even swung around a few times on the way out to make sure nobody followed as I rushed to catch up with him, cutting through an alley to another street. Nobody would find us.

"You make out good back there?" I said laughing, slapping his arm.

"What are you talking about?"

"I saw everything. Everything!"

"Yeah?"

"Yeah."

"Drinks on me for the rest of the night," He replied with a smirk.

"Can't believe you did that. I could never do that."

"You got a job. No reason why you would ever be taking a risk like this. I don't have that option to work, and I'd lose my check if I did. This is a lot for me. I need it. Besides, this is dumb stuff. I'm ashamed I even did that."

"I'm not cut out for crime and never have been. I think I'm quitting Uptown Dogs real soon. Lee is getting to be a real bitch and I've almost had it. I'm ready to get back into construction again."

"You must have some serious scratch saved or you're a fool to leave a job like that. You get paid to walk dogs, how easy is that? And those guys like you, too. Don't fuck that up."

I didn't like to talk about money with Tony because I did have a decent chunk put aside. I felt as though he would take it if he could get to it. He would try to manipulate it out of me or just keep asking for loans, not intentionally, but out of habit to support his addiction, until I was drained. That's how his mind is programmed after all these years. As long as I lived with him he'd feel like he could, because he had that power over me. The majority of the reason I could save like I did was because my overhead was so low, due to living with him, but I didn't want him knowing that and expecting more from me.

"You got it easy, Tony; free apartment, checks from the government, food stamps, and god knows what else they give you. And you do whatever you want, whenever you want. I work seven days a week and I can't afford anything better than your couch unless I move way out in the boroughs. It's not fair."

"Seven days a week? They got you working on the weekends? Thought they were closed."

I stuttered for a second as I tried to find an answer to why I didn't tell him about Betty.

"Yeah, it's just some cleanup around the shop and filing, nothing big, just short of a full day. They pay shit anyway."

"Sure they do. You're probably loaded."

For a second I thought maybe he knew I was lying. Maybe he was smart enough to try to confuse me. He always seemed to know more than he let on, but most of it was a hunch. A liar like him knew better than to believe anyone. But it was still none of his business and he knew it, and he didn't care either way.

"And, not for nothing, but I don't want any of the free money I get. I don't wanna suck off the system like I do. I never wanted that for myself. I used to be a worker like you."

It was late already. Some of the bars were closing and people were walking home. We went back to the park and he stopped at a bench to empty his pockets and see what he got. Tony counted the money: $400. He even lifted two iPhones and a white gold necklace with a diamond pendant that was in a velvet pouch. He seemed pleased and threw me forty bucks for "looking out" he said. His eyes bulged as he snooped through the unlocked phone, going through the photos and texts. He showed me a few pictures and we laughed. She had some sexy selfies she took in the mirror and they were pretty goofy, but I got excited looking at them and grabbed the phone to get a closer view. The other photos were mostly her and her boyfriend, who looked like a square. Kind of felt wrong going through someone's personal stuff like that, but it was fun.

Tony was now saying he could crash, and I wanted to go home, too. He wasted no time reading my mind and handed me two white, pills, said it would knock me out fast. I knew already I'd feel like shit tomorrow, but I'd make it through.

We walked back home as the pills began to take hold, my legs growing heavier and heavier with each step. Those girls wouldn't be missing anything they can't replace. They'd only spend it on material stuff, just as much as an addiction as Tony's substances. I felt bad but it wasn't personal and they'd get over it. I'd probably be upset if it happened to me, and it has. That which can be stolen or taken might have never really belonged to us in the first place. I didn't like that he did it, and I didn't like knowing about it, but I brushed it off as I did with all his crookedness, because he was my friend and I accepted him. At the end of the day, no matter the dishonesty, cheating ways, and drug use, I still thought highly of him. It didn't change the way I felt about him, or make me forget all his unique qualities. He was there for me when I needed, helped me get off the streets, and accepted me, too. Tony got a pack of smokes and a few Little Debbie cakes for us. He was quiet, for a change, so I was surprised when he said,

"You don't talk much, do ya, Johny? You never ask many questions or anything."

After a long hesitation I answered.

"These days I just wait for people to talk to me."

"I like it. Too many people I know can't stop running their mouths, talking crap. If I could keep my mouth shut then I would, it's gotten me in a lot of trouble."

"Man, I don't even know what to say anymore. Look at my life. There isn't much to share. You got stories, Tony, I don't, not like yours at least. I feel boring next to you."

It was true. I didn't have much to say, nothing presentable at least. I had no drive anymore to talk about things, myself, issues, or anything else. I didn't know much about anything nor have I been anywhere. It made people nervous, but the ones who didn't overthink it were the ones I made friends with.

"Don't say that, pal. You ain't boring. You're private and I like that, makes me feel safe. Tell me about this Sara girl you were living with in Brooklyn. What's she doing now?"

"Who knows. I was thinking of visiting her a few times at the café she was working at, but I can't bring myself to do it. She'd probably just look at me in disgust or have some new boyfriend behind the counter with her. She got her revenge on me, that's for sure. If I saw her I don't even know if she'd say hi, slap me, or ignore me."

"I'm very familiar with the wrath of exes..." started Tony.

I didn't reply so he kept going. I wanted to hear this.

"In fact, just last year I had my girl of four years up and leave me for this other guy, some total idiot. Every time I tried to talk to her and see her, she acted like it was harassment, and threatened to call the cops a few times if I wouldn't leave her alone. It was crazy. I was nothing but a gentleman to her. They're still together now, and supposedly she's happy, so I've heard. That's hard for me to believe, though. I hate to say it, but I never felt like there was much hope for her. She was always looking for the next person to hang on to for a comfortable ride. She didn't have much feeling about anything, and I saw that in the end in how she dropped me so coldly. It was all a lie with her and she wasted no time moving to the next."

When he told me this, I actually wondered how much truth there was to it. So many guys, including myself, change the story to make ourselves seem innocent, leaving out necessary details. We claim the girl goes crazy on us, but deep down we know we're at least half, if not more, to blame. He could have been lying and cheating, or maybe he went on one too many benders, she left him, and he went nuts. Or maybe she was just looking for the next ride, like he said. Didn't matter anyway. She discarded him like Sara discarded me, and we knew it was coming.

"I've had my problems with women, too, but I can't say it wasn't my fault to some degree. I've been a straight up asshole to a lot of chicks. I don't even know why. I get bored really fast."

"Me too. When I had loads of money, I used to always keep as many girls as I could on the back burner, just in case I had to line up the next thing. I never really put much effort into any of them. Let too many nice ones give up on me." He replied.

"So, how'd you get this job walking dogs anyway? Did you know those two or is this something you'd been doing?"

"No. I just walked in one day and asked if they were hiring. I'd been searching for a job for months and nothing. I figured I might as well ask. Nothing else was working."

"You're lucky, Johny. People still give you chances because you look normal. If I thought I could get a real job, I would try to get clean. Everyone knows I'm beyond that point. I can't even walk in the supermarket without getting followed like I'm gonna shoplift."

"It's hardly a real job. I'm sleeping on your couch, Tony. I don't have any security there. A least you got government support for life as a safety net."

"What I get from the government is chump change, and it makes me feel bad and has made me weak. They got me, for life, just like an addiction. I'm chained and feel like shit about it. I wish I had a regular life and job. Other times I think I'd go crazy if I did. I have no idea what I want but now I'm stuck on their mouse wheel."

"Neither do I. If I knew what I wanted, things would be different."

It was true. I'd never had any direction, and neither had he. Could I blame that on my mom? No. It was everything. It's just the way things turned out, and people like us are lost byproducts of a screwed up system.

"You got any kids?" He seemed like the type that would, so I asked. I'd been curious for a while.

He slowed for a moment and glanced at me real serious. His eyes looked teary. For a 'tough' guy, Tony teared up a lot, especially when he was talking about his mom or some past stuff, but that was as far as it ever got. I wondered why he did the things he did only to feel so horrible about them later.

"Yeah. I got two kids, twin girls, Emily and Carla. Seven years old. Haven't seen them in five years, but I've tried. My ex is married to this guy who thinks he's the dad now, and they won't let me around. They think it will just confuse the girls. When I got out of the can, I tried to get everything back that I had before, the money, the car, the nice apartment, the family, and start over, but my ex just wanted to punish me for hurting her and getting arrested, like I did it on purpose or something. She felt like I abandoned her and found someone else. I tried to see the kids, but she made it impossible, and had so much shit on me that I couldn't take her to court. But, that's another story for another time, if ever."

"I'm real sorry about that. They'll get older and want to see you on their own. I bet they're wondering about you now."

He didn't say anything and I knew he couldn't. I don't think he'd ever get his shit together enough to see them while they were still young. Maybe one day they would seek him out, or he'd be allowed to meet them and they'd find him to be some scary stranger, and they'd be happy he hadn't been around to ruin their young years. Or maybe they'd love him. I hoped they would love him.

We were silent the rest of the way.

The pills kicked in fully right before we got back, and it hit me hard with the alcohol in my system. I can't remember how I fell asleep, but the next morning I woke sitting upright still in my sneakers. I walked out the door like that. I could clean up at the shop and change my clothes. It was early so I took my time heading in.

Friday was a humid, drizzly day. Not many people were out and it was a relief. I stopped to take some pictures of the smoke stacks and the fog around the buildings using this new cell phone I got the week before. The last phone was old and outdated, but this one was like a mini computer and I was playing around with it most the time. Taking pictures was never my thing before because I never had a camera in my life. I snapped away like I was committing a crime, afraid of looking like a tourist, looking around making sure nobody was watching me. The beauty of my pictures captivated me. They were mine. It was the first attempt at being artistic in my life.

My head was pounding, so I stopped to get a coffee and pop an Advil. I sat at a table and started spacing out, not wanting to go into work and not wanting to see Sandra, or deal with the stress of it.

Thoughts of the night before ran through my head. I was worried about Tony. I relied on him for a place to live, but also as my only companion, and I didn't want him to get busted or have a heart attack from all the drugs. I know a guy like him will die young, and he'll never get to see his kids. He'll never stop. I hoped he'd be around long enough to be there for me when I needed him. It sounded selfish, but it wasn't. I just wanted him to be around as long as he could be.

I started to fall into a sleep and I caught myself. If I slept I'd catch up, but everything else would fall behind. I wanted to call my mom, but couldn't bring myself to do it. I'd do it later. She talked and I never had anything to say, and I never had anything I wanted to tell her. We had nothing in common anymore, if ever, and she knew nothing of my life here. I never invited her to visit. I kept avoiding her, though soon I knew I had to find a way to get closer, when I could be consistent.

The day was hell to get through. The first pass in front of the mirror was nothing short of a shock. Rough nights go right to your face when you're in your thirties, and I looked like I had aged twenty years overnight.

"Johny, you look awful today. What happened to you?" Lee asked when he came in and glanced at me, looking stunned.

I just stared at him and shook my head. He understood what that meant.

"Oh no. I hope you're still going on that date with Sandra!"

"Yeah, I'm still gonna go, but I won't be out late. I don't think she'll forgive me if I back out the same day."

"I'm sure she'd understand if you had to cancel, but that wouldn't be a good start and you'd hurt her. Just get a bite and go home, sleep it off. First dates are best light anyway."

I was jealous of Tony, who got to sleep it off in bed. When I left I saw him sprawled on his mattress as usual, with his legs hanging off. He'd probably sleep all day. He had these torn and dusty American flags over the basement windows, keeping it dark in there, a coffin for the jobless vampire that he is. When he wakes he'll be ready to forget his grief on his next run.

The day rolled by and I began to feel better. Sandra came in to drop off Bella and I was able to keep myself together. We confirmed we'd meet outside after I finished work, and I saw her again later when she picked up Bella. When the time grew closer, my stomach grew more and more uneasy. It overwhelmed me so much that I was tempted to tell her something came up.

"Hi," was all I managed to say to her as I walked outside, my heart racing.

"Hello," was all she managed to say back. I could hear in her voice that she was also nervous. The day was over, and the date had begun.

Looking out to the park, she stood with her back facing me. When she turned around and our eyes met, it was a difficult moment — the main reason why I hated dating. But I pushed through it quickly, because she looked beautiful. She had makeup on and was dressed in a nice outfit, nothing fancy but better than usual. She must have changed for me. We both started talking to break the silence. I told her to speak first, and she told me it was nothing and that I should talk. We laughed, which eased the tension. I asked her about her day, and that led to asking where she lived, and how working for Bobby and Shelly, Bella's owners, was going. They all seemed like routine questions, because I didn't know anything much about her. She asked me some questions, too. None of them I wanted to answer, especially the one about where I live and with whom, to which I replied;

"Not far, uptown more. It's just me and this guy, who rents an extra room out to me. He's not around much."

One thing would be certain, I would never take her back there and she would never meet Tony.

"I live uptown, too," she said. "It's an old house that belonged to my grandparents."

"Oh, so you live with your family still?"

I felt her get uncomfortable and I regretted using the word "still."

"Well, yeah, but it's just my mom and sisters and brother and we pay rent to my mom. I think it's better than renting and easier to save. Plus, I wouldn't be able to afford to live in that area, so it works out better."

She sounded embarrassed to be living at home.

"I'd do the same thing if my mom lived in the city. No sense throwing all your money away on rent when you have that situation right here."

We continued to talk, but I wasn't really listening to the conversation. Looking at her up-close in the light, she appeared older than I thought she was, but it was hard to tell. I think I was overanalyzing. Her teeth were a bit more yellow than I noticed before, and her skin rougher than normal, which she tried to hide with extra makeup.

Sometimes I'd see her flaws as we were talking and I'd get shy, hoping she didn't see me scanning her like that. I was searching her face. And I kept searching, because she had an interesting depth to her. Her flaws weren't flaws to me. I wasn't like those guys looking for a pin up. They were part of her authenticity and I was attracted to her. I hope she knew that.

"Where are we walking?" she asked.

"I don't know."

I was about to try and find out what she wanted to do, watch a movie or grab a bite, but she started talking again. I wasn't aware she was such a talker. Maybe it was nerves.

Once she finished I would interject and try to figure something out. I didn't want to walk for hours. I was still tired and just wanted to get home and sleep.

"So, we're going to the movies, right?" she said, looking at me.

"Yeah, sure, if that's what you wanna do. I'm game. Did you look it up last night? You know what's playing?"

"Didn't get a chance to find out. I got busy."

She looked at me and it turned me on. I bet she didn't want to go to the movies. I had the feeling she wanted to sit somewhere, talk, and try to get close to me. I'd rather that, too, but I wouldn't let it happen just yet. At least neither of us is prepared.

She went on to say; "I'm cool with anything, even if we get something to eat and bring it in the park. We can swing by the movies, too, if you want. There's a place to eat nearby that's supposed to be good."

I hesitated to answer, and could tell she was growing fearful as a result. She tried to pass it off, thinking I wouldn't reply. It seemed too long a pause, but then I grabbed her hand and told her I knew a really nice place. Something finally popped in my mind. She followed my lead, her clammy hand clenching mine.

We walked quickly and quietly. I could have led her to at least five places in the park that I knew she'd like, but I remembered this one spot Tony took me to a while back. It was a hotel overlooking the park and there was a trick to getting on the roof that Tony knew of. I would have to try to remember the secret way up for this to work.

At Central Park West I recognized the building and we turned the corner to enter the loading dock. A few guys were sitting there, but did nothing as we strolled straight to the elevator. I pushed the button to the sixtieth floor, and that was it. She kept asking where we were going and I told her it was a surprise. When we got to the top we reached a staircase and walked two more flights to the roof. The door had a combination lock and my heart sank when I saw it, and she saw it too, but I touched it and it opened. It had never been fastened shut. It was exactly the same when Tony took me.

The sky was full of pinks and oranges. It reflected off every building in the city like a mirror. When Tony brought me here it was dark and the city was full of lights, but right now with Sandra, as the sun was going down, it was something right out of a postcard. I wanted to touch her, as premature as I thought it would be. It felt the moment for something spontaneous and intimate. Something brought us together, then here to show us all of this. And everything felt right.

As we sat watching the city go from pink to blue, blue to gray, and gray to black, with artificial lights that looked like stars growing brighter all around us, I thought of kissing her more and more. It had been so long and I missed the touch of a woman and the feeling of a kiss, the feeling of new love. We neared the edge and she let go of my hand to stand as close as possible, peering down. I made sure to stand next to her in case she lost her footing.

The date was going better than I could have imagined. There was no pressure to talk over such a view. We separately explored the roof, as though we were on the summit of a mountain. She walked over to me and stood. It got so silent that in some urgency to break it I clasped her hand, drew her body to mine, and kissed her. Our lips were mismatched in the beginning, but once they began folding into each other perfectly, she pulled away. I think she felt the same frightening intensity that I did.

I squeezed her waist momentarily before letting go and said we should get something to eat. She followed my lead again, though I didn't know where to take her, or what she expected. I wondered if I should pay or if she was the type to insist on paying half, and if I should let her. Perhaps she would tell me the kind of place she liked, and I hoped it wouldn't be too expensive.

But we walked and talked for over an hour, and I forgot my hunger and realized that she was leading me somewhere.

"I live close to here. There is a falafel place around the corner that just opened, if you want to go. I haven't been there yet but my sister says it's good."

Falafel. She likes that kind of food. I'm the kind of guy who lives on junk; pizza, subs, bagels.

"Yeah, I love falafel. Let's go there," I lied.

It wasn't that I didn't like falafel and hummus and all that stuff, I just wasn't ever in the mood for that kind of food, because I saw it more as a side plate rather than a meal. But I wanted to go where she wanted to go. I wanted her to be happy.

"Where did you grow up?" she asked.

"A small city south of Boston. It's not really a great place. I've been living here for a while now, though."

"I've never been to Boston but I've heard it's pretty. Maybe one of these days I'll take the bus up. There are ones that leave from Chinatown and they're only ten dollars each way."

"Hahaha. Yea, take those buses at your own risk. They drive crazy, but they'll get you there fast. If you go soon, let me know, and I'll give you some tips."

The falafel place was casual. I insisted on paying and she had no qualms about it. She took five minutes to order, asked a million questions, and wanted to know the ingredients — if there was dairy in this or that. I got the sense that she was not only a picky eater, but also one of those types that couldn't, or wouldn't, eat regular food. Before I had the chance to ask, she told me that she's 'veg,' whatever that meant, and laughed, as if worried that telling me this might completely turn me off. In a way it did, just because I didn't want to be judged for what I ate around someone like this or deal with her long list of preferences. I brushed it off.

She had this funny way of devouring food as though she were starving. She even reached for a few of my pita chips, which shocked me, especially since she had asked for no pita chips with her order, which came free with her plate. I found myself taken aback by her odd table graces, but I guess I just wasn't obsessed with eating as much as she was, so I let her finish the rest of my chips. I'd eat something on the way home if I were still hungry. She also got very talkative and was laughing a lot, covering her mouth as she did, rather than taking a break from her food for a few moments. It was awkward, but somehow turned me on to her more.

After dinner I felt worn out and just wanted to go to sleep, preferably on my couch, but I'd even crash on a bench if I had to, on the grass, or anywhere for a nap. My legs could hardly move. I even told her about the night before and hanging out until late with my roommate, told her all but the drugs and stealing part. She said I could sleep at her place if I wanted, on the couch of course. As much as I wanted to, I couldn't, I declined and headed back to Tony's, hoping we could pick up where we left off another time. It's always so hard to know. Things can turn at the drop of a hat, and sometimes you don't know how, can't take something back, or are too afraid to make the next move, if you should. Then, before you know it, you fade or fall apart, lose contact, misunderstand the situation, get scared, cease communication. I could tell when we said goodbye that she was afraid of the same thing. If I had the courage to kiss her again I would have, but I panicked and withdrew quickly. All I could say as I walked away was,

"I'd like to do this again."

She blushed and replied, "For sure."

She is so nice. I thought of her the whole way home.

*****

Life is long when I'm waiting, and I fear I've spent most of my life waiting and losing so much time in the process. Life is short when you are where you want to be, but nothing lasts. Somewhere in the middle of gaining and losing, we are always closer to losing, or letting go. I'm terrified to grow old alone, and it's on my mind so often that I have nightmares about my hair turning gray and falling out, and sometimes even my teeth. I have no glory days to speak of, and now the time has come and gone. Some of my hairs are already gray. I wondered if Betty felt the same way or has become used to it. I'm new to this feeling, but I hope it gets easier, or that's it's imagined and will depart as I enter a better stage in my life.

This Saturday morning Betty looked extra tired. Every day she looked as though she lost a little bit more than the day before. But I couldn't help finding her increasingly graceful. The picture in the hall was exactly how I saw her.

And despite her sagging skin and white hair, she was still beautiful.

While Jack and I were out for a walk it started to rain and we ran back early. I had nowhere to be, so, like most days, I hung around at Betty's with Jack, her, and Harvey. It was comfortable between us. I played with Jack a lot and he was starting to stay by my side. Betty didn't mind and looked rather content about it. She loved him, but I could see she didn't have the energy for him at all, especially on the days where she was weak.

Harvey was in and out, running errands and making phone calls while Betty went back and forth from her desk to her bedroom, napping, reading, and at times watching me and Jack. She loved to read and always had a newspaper or magazine that Harvey left for her in the morning. After she finished, she would bring what she was reading over to me so that I could read it, too. Though I wasn't interested, I pretended to be, even pretending to read said periodicals.

Today there was a violin case in the corner.

"Is that your violin, Betty? Can you play?"

"A long time ago. I was actually quite good. This morning I had the desire to play at 6 a.m. I have no idea why, but then I brought it in here and forgot what I was going to do. Old age," she replied with a laugh. "Maybe I was sleepwalking."

She plucked Jack off her lap and placed him on the floor, then wheeled herself over to the case. While slowly reaching for it, she moaned. I wanted to go over and help her pick it up but she motioned for me to stay put. When it was finally on her lap, she took the violin from the case, tightened the bow, and tried it. The sound that emanated was sweet, like nothing I'd ever heard before. I watched her intently, with adoration, even as her hand got too wobbly and she couldn't hold it anymore. The ten seconds she played were not long enough and I wanted to hear more, but she put it on her lap. She looked at it lovingly and stroked the wood, held it before her for a minute, then put it back in the case. I wanted to say something consoling, but was afraid it would just sound like sympathy.

"I would love to play, but it was a long time ago that I did, before you were born, I'm sure. This old violin can play again, but I can't, and it's as out of tune as I feel. I will donate it to someone who needs and deserves a fine instrument such as this. It's time for this violin's next life. Remind me to tell Harvey."

"Of course." I replied.

She said everything today with a forced smile, as she always did when she was exhausted and in pain. Again we sat in silence. I really do love Betty. In my mind I said it to myself and was surprised I could feel this way about her, but not in a way where I want to be her lover, just in a way where I felt this connection with her, of how she found me and came into my life so abruptly — and fortuitously. Nobody had ever found me like she had.

Last night with Sandra was on my mind. I could see her in my head again, standing in front of the pink sunset as I kissed her. She is too pure for me and I'm not sure I deserve her. I don't know what I'm going to do with her, but I can't stop myself from going forward with her.

"Johny..." Betty started, and I couldn't tell if she wanted to ask me something or if she was just uttering my name the way old people sometimes blurt things out. Perhaps she forgot what she wanted to say, as she often does. After some time she continued.

"Johny... I want to ask you a few things, but sometimes I lack tact and don't want to pry."

I must have had a look of approval, because she glanced at me and seemed satisfied enough to proceed.

"How old are you, Johny?"

"I'm 36, going on 37 in November. Why?"

"So, what do you really want out of life? More to the point, where do you see yourself in five or ten years?"

These were questions I didn't like, because there were no answers, because I had no answers, because I knew these questions were loaded with expectations. They were judgments to fit me into a mold, or some idea of social worth. I don't have life goals other than finding happiness. Unfocused answers like that are never good enough for those who ask such things. I have no plan to speak of, no need to prove anything, and that is noble in my eyes.

"I don't know where I'll be in ten years. Ten years ago I never imagined where my life would be now. I prefer to live in the moment," I said.

That was all I could say. It was quiet for about ten seconds, and then she shrugged and made a face that looked like she accepted the frankness of my answer. Rejection, hardships, and lack of opportunity were very real elements in my life. I wanted to tell her I felt ambitious, but there's no proof of it. I didn't know my passions and am afraid to admit I wanted more but didn't believe in myself. Hopefully, wherever I'll be, it's somewhere better than I am now.

"I don't see a path right now. Maybe it will come to me. I don't know how to answer this question, Betty. I suppose what is meant to happen, will happen."

"Yes, yes, but it's okay to set goals and accomplish them in time, Johny. We all want to have the things we like and to earn them, and that's in your power to create it. Whether you want to be comfortable or you want to be filthy rich, it's okay, but no need to give up because life takes unexpected turns or things don't go your way. That can be a good thing. I'm just asking because, if you have something that interests you, or an idea, then now is the time to figure it out and find a way to pursue it. The older you get, the harder it gets — so much harder. Don't be afraid to fail. What other people think is unimportant. I can help you if you need. If there is something you want to do, an education, a business, just tell me. I want to be here for you and see you do well. You deserve it, and I have a feeling your life hasn't been easy."

She was spot on. I didn't want to think or be reminded of the fact that I was a habitual quitter. The truth was, I didn't know how to make anything happen. She had no clue how difficult it is for the rest of us, people like Tony and me. But maybe, just maybe, I'm making excuses not to try. Maybe my scapegoats are self-imposed obstacles to remain a child. Her thoughtfulness towards me touched me deeply, and I didn't know how to express that, not that she needed me to. I felt myself getting angry, but knew that was just a defense mechanism. I wish everyone understood me like she does.

"You're right. I need to think of something for my future. It's been on my mind a lot and the time is coming soon where I'll figure it out. Don't know what, just yet, but I'll let you know if and when I need help. Thank you." And I meant it. I would try. I would think of it.

Betty came over to me and reached her hand to touch my arm.

"It's none of my business. I found that in life it's always better to let someone figure things out for themselves. It will come to you in time. It comes to all of us eventually. Sometimes we just need a hand to move forward."

"It's all right, Betty. Thank you."

I wasn't bothered. Her eyes looked innocent, pink lids over blue marbles, and her frail hands felt so soft touching mine for that moment. She backed up and stared at the painting across the room on the other wall, with her bony body humped forward in the wheelchair, her green dress falling around her concave shoulders, and her tight bun falling to the side as her head tilted. It was a large-scale landscape painting in a gold frame, old and most certainly valuable, the type you'd see in an aristocrat's castle. There were a few like this one in the hall downstairs that I'd seen before, but this one was bigger. The setting depicted was lush green, with a purple sunset and big weeping willow trees. Small figures, which looked like English gentlemen with their dogs, seemed to be contemplating enlightening ideas, the idea of discovering America perhaps. Betty stared at it and saw nothing. It was so familiar to her that it served only as a focal point. Her eyes indicated thought, but the rest of her turned pale and suddenly she lost her ability to sit up straight, letting out a long sigh that sounded more like a last breath. If it weren't for the sunlight revealing her rosy cheeks, I would have thought her near dead already. This was usually how she fell asleep.

I picked up the newspaper and proceeded to read a few articles with little interest. Her faint snoring grew louder and louder, and I figured this would be a good time to leave her in peace for her nap. She didn't like to be woken and preferred sleeping in her chair just as she was. I rose and attached Jack's leash, proceeding out without a word. I thought she would die while we were gone on our walk and I got so sad. I told Harvey she was in there and he said that he'd wake her for her snack later.

I thought of her words earlier. Nobody ever offered to help me before in my life. I thought about it and, although I knew I'd never ask her for anything, I wanted to make her proud. She was there when I returned, looking better and chatting with Harvey.

*****

At the end of summer, I left my job with Chris and Lee. Although I needed every penny I could get, I just couldn't go back. They wondered what happened to me, called my phone a bunch of times, and then likely assumed I'd moved on. I was upset at myself that I gave no notice. One day Betty called to see if I could come by early and I just decided to go there instead, since the pay was better, and I knew she wanted me full time. Early voicemails Lee left sounded angry, the last few were worried, and then he wished me well, "no hard feelings, hope you're alright. I don't understand why you couldn't have told us." As usual, Chris was mum. He left no messages, said nothing, and probably assumed I got fed up with Lee, as he had too. He was rarely around during the last few months there. What they liked least about my being gone was that they had to do the work themselves. Towards the end, Lees' behavior was careless. The problems he was having with Chris made him act spitefully, and I felt he took it out on me. Sandra told me it took them weeks to find someone else, a young kid who didn't have much of a personality, and in that time they were running around like madmen. Never once did they approach Sandra to ask about me. I told her I couldn't take Lee anymore, and she understood. She had noticed it, too.

 I don't know why I left them like that. They had done a lot for me, taking me on at a time when I really needed a chance. I got spoiled at Betty's and, apart from disliking Lee, I grew out of Uptown Dogs. They refused my request for a raise a while back, claiming that times were tough at the moment, but possibly down the road we could revisit it. I resented that. I felt like I was getting underpaid considering I took on all the duties there. More than likely it was Lees' decision, but Chris agreed to everything as well. Now I was making better money at Betty's full time and life had taken a new turn. I was sorry I burned my bridges with them, but I hoped I'd never need to go back. I think they are used to people coming and going from that job.

Sandra and I grew close in a short time and, after a few months, I was sure I loved her — though I didn't let on. We spent most evenings together and I started sleeping at her house some nights. She always wanted to be with me. It sometimes became overwhelming and I needed my space, but my distance just made her chase me harder. She would text me first thing in the morning, at lunchtime, and right before I finished work. You'd think she never fell in love before. But, I liked it. It made me fall in love with her, which scared me. She didn't need to play games, be a bitch, be unavailable, or be perfect, to get my love and respect. All she needed was to be her funny, sweet, self.

There was still so much I had to hide about my life and who I was, and this made me reluctant to be completely open. I kept most everything to myself, and so much of what I did tell her was a lie. But, it was for her own benefit. I could never recount the details with Sara or other past relationships. She'd be terrified I'd do the same to her. There was no need to know the past, or the truth, whatever that was. She knew me in all ways that count and could trust me.

Almost half the week I stayed at Sandra's, just because she wanted me to, and it was better to be with her than in Tony's bunker. Every time we got together we would end up back at her place for the night. It was convenient, and now that we were having sex, that's all we wanted to do.

The one drawback to her house was her family. They might be the weirdest family I've ever encountered. Sandra said they didn't have much money, but they lived in a brownstone high up in the upper west side, which was worth a fortune in spite of being completely rundown. Sandra's uncle, a wealthy man, kept far from their family while handling the taxes and other expenses needed for them to stay there. It had been in the family for generations and had sentimental value to him. There was probably more to the story than that, but that's all I was told.

Everything inside the house was old, probably belonging to her grandparents, or even her great grandparents. Rugs were ragged and worn down to threads in some spots, carefully covering broken pieces of wood on the floors. The paint on the walls was chipping, and it looked like they had sloppily re-painted layers over layers over beautiful woodwork and formerly exposed brick. The staircase had half a railing missing. The place had so much potential, yet it looked like a rickety haunted house. All the furniture was ripped and discolored from age. Everything was dusty and smelled like an attic. Nothing changed in this house, not for a long time. Some things were neglected, not for lack of money, but out of sheer laziness.

Sandra complained about her job so much that I realized she had no work ethic. She thought she was being taken advantage of by the couple she worked for and was underpaid. I told her if that's how she felt then she should quit, but she would say she couldn't do that because she loved Bella too much. It was like she didn't want an option, just to complain. Her moods were on and off, proud to humble, insecure to secure, ungrateful to grateful. I never knew what to expect or how to keep up because she often changed her mind. When I sensed she was in a state, I tried to be quiet and agree with all she said, waiting for it to pass. A few times she had blown up at me claiming I didn't care about her. I walked out and, of course, she chased after me apologetically. I felt confused and attracted to her at the same time. I knew in time her rough edges would smooth out, and they did. She never got close to anyone before and just needed some time to adjust. She loved me so much and I didn't know how to handle it, but I decided to just go with it, because I felt the same way about her.

As far as Sandra's job, there were few opportunities that would pay as much as that couple and, as far as I knew, all she did was putter around all day or run menial errands, do some minor cleaning, and, of course, dropping off and picking up Bella. When she got bored she sent me texts, long ones, many with pictures of the cat she was playing with or something she thought was cute, but I didn't answer much of them. I didn't want to encourage unsustainable back and forth, especially when I barely looked at my phone. I'm not big on texting that is not utilitarian. Despite the fact that I didn't respond, she sent them, as though she were talking to herself. The only ones I replied to were texts that actually had a concrete question about meeting up somewhere after work or another plan. I think she also knew it was too much, but couldn't help herself.

There were times Sandra smelled like the old house. There were times she did not look beautiful or even pretty, though she was. There were times she dressed unfeminine, talked loudly, and acted flaky. The clothes she wore, mostly black and gray, always looked tattered, which was odd because her mother and sisters dressed typical of Manhattan women — classy, and sexy. Sandra dressed with no definable style, but she had her own special way. And, I saw she was trying to look better, on my account. She went shopping and burrowed her sister's clothes. Sometimes it worked, sometimes she looked funny, but she made me laugh, anyway.

And it wasn't just me thinking this. Others were judging her. I noticed the looks she got when we'd go out to eat and on the subway, especially when she was speaking. She had a way of talking, an accent that was like nothing I'd recognized. I'd heard it when I first met her but dismissed it. And many times her conversation sounded peculiar and she'd talk about herself for too long, not making much sense. People always noticed her and looked as though they didn't quite know what to think, same as what I thought in our first meeting. Her look was dark and exotic yet her personality was nervous, warm, and clumsy, not what one would expect at first sight. She got underestimated a lot, and she knew it. If only she had more confidence in herself then her outwardly impression could improve. I felt that I needed to be very gentle with her on account of that, and whatever happened in her life to make her doubt herself so much. The way I saw it was that she just needed a little love, and she was worth it to me.

At times, however, I wished she were more like other girls in some respects, though. Or, rather, I wished she were more like other women. I wished she were more sure of herself. If she had been married, had kids, lived anywhere else at one time, or had a career, perhaps she would have grown out of her immaturity sooner. But if she were anything more I wouldn't be good enough for her, and perhaps she knew it. We were both projects for each other in many respects. I saw her as an empty palette that was soon to be something even greater.

Sandra's siblings were all younger; 21, 23, 26, 29 and 33. None of them had ever moved out. The 33-year-old, Sam, seemed to have a good job in banking, always in a nice suit when he came home, and a likable guy. His room looked like a 15-year-old inhabited it; Yankees memorabilia mixed with pinups. There were flags and posters all over the walls, postcard art, a black curtain that kept out most of the daylight, a huge plasma TV, and a closest full of impeccably pressed suits. Sam was friendly when we met. I noticed his perfectly aligned white teeth right away. The rest of Sandra's siblings, or at least the other girls, weren't so social with me. They seemed surprised that I was with her, and seemed surprised I wasn't hitting on them. At one time or another I felt them flirt with me in a way that was rude to Sandra, but I never fell for it.

Edward was the youngest and, at 21, he looked as if he were 17. He was always in baggy clothes, hair to his shoulders and lots of piercings. He and Sandra were a lot alike, and he was the only one in the house she seemed close to. The two of them talked and laughed together more than any of the others, and they made dinner together a lot. The other three sisters mocked them constantly, especially in front of me. After all, the girls were snobs and Sandra and Eddie were as far from that as could be.

Nobody bothered Sam, and I think it's because they all relied on him for money here and there, since he was the only real breadwinner in the house. He was neutral, didn't communicate with them much, and was barely around. I'm sure he wanted to move out, but was somehow attached to this place and the lure of cheap rent.

The other girls, Darryl, Diane, and Darcy, were always together, getting manicures or shopping, coming home with bags, trying to pass off looking like they were shopping on Fifth Avenue when they were at the knockoff stores. That appeared to be all they did or cared about, shop, go on dates, and be on their phone for hours.

The entire family was wild. I was convinced the mother, Stella, was flighty like her 3-D daughters — that's how Sandra referred to them. I'd seen Stella with at least three different men in the parlor, drinking, smoking her fancy cigarettes, and laughing loudly every time a joke was told. Sandra was embarrassed of her. She went on dates with guys that were either much younger or much older, but I never saw her intimate with anyone nor do I believe she was. I'd say she does it to amuse herself into believing she still has the power of beauty and seduction to wield, and she does. For a woman in her late fifties, she looked like a movie star that had scarcely aged. I was puzzled that she managed to raise six children, by herself for the last 5 years. The father lived in the city but Sandra never talked to him much. She said he looked down on them, everyone except Sammy, and that he had a new life with a high society woman he met years ago and never came around to say hello or contribute anything to their lives.

If it weren't for that house and their uncle, everyone except for Sam would be lost. Nobody paid any mind when I started living there part-time, because nobody really cared. The house could be full or empty and they'd remain the same, constantly bickering with one another like children. No one put on airs or extra manners on my account.

And the house had no official or unofficial rules for guest like me. According to Sandra, there had been many friends, relatives, and boyfriends that slept on the couch for months at a time. If someone wanted to plant themselves there, they certainly could. But the place was too chaotic for anyone to stand more than was absolutely necessary.

Sandra's sisters and mother always tried to engage me in these conversations where Sandra wasn't involved. They even tried to gang up on Sandra in front of me a few times and bring up humiliating stories of her past, to which she would shake her head at them. In their shameless attempts to try and make her feel badly, they only made themselves look wretched. I don't think they meant to be mean, but they just didn't know any better and were trying to be funny. I'd like to think they felt sorry after, but who knows if they did. I was happy to be an only child for once in my life. Nevertheless, they were beginning to feel like family, and I became fond of them, to the unruliness of the house, and to all of their imperfect personalities, the good and the bad. It wasn't long until I had completely moved in and forgot about Tony's altogether.

It was a hot September afternoon. I left Betty's and returned home before Sandra. I sat on the parlor couch, waiting for a while before going through a dusty record collection that sat in boxes on the floor, probably belonging to her late grandmother. I decided to explore, discovering old jazz albums— Billie Holiday, Louis Armstrong, Charlie Parker, and Chet Baker, among others. An old gramophone that looked like it might still work sat beside the stack. I don't think it was an antique, as it had a contemporary plug.

Stella wobbled in looking like she was on a stronger-than-usual cocktail of Valium and gin, holding her glass high and stirring the ice with her straw. Her perfume nauseated me, contaminating the air and giving me an instant headache. I sensed trouble, but kept my head down, sorting through the pile of music, trying to appear as though I was involved in the task. Sometimes I wished she would leave me alone, but here I was in her house, forced to listen to her stories and entertain her whims, just like all the other men in her life. The luxury I had of being alone while living at Tony's was missed at times.

She strolled over, twirling in the center of the room, demanding instant attention. She wanted my acknowledgement.

"Hi, Johny. The gramophone was restored years back. It works if you're interested in playing some of those records."

She sunk into the large chair in the middle of the room, watching me the entire time without moving her eyes, her heels barely able to stay grounded on the floor. It was where she always sat. The yellow satin chair had thin red and blue stripes, and was probably very nice at one time, until the parade of stray cats that entered the house got to it and used it as a scratching post. This house was a free-for-all for every stray cat in a five-block radius. They came and went through the broken windows in the basement. Most of the time they warmed up or cooled off down there without coming upstairs, and took advantage of the food and water Sandra and her mom left out in large bowls. A few friendly ones ascended occasionally, making themselves at home on the cushy furniture. They were the housecats. The smell of cat pee was the first thing I noticed about this place when I walked in.

The sight of Stella made me want to laugh and I smiled. I started to choke on this sensation, then swallowed it and tried to think of something serious. She looked charming, sitting there with heavy eyelids, makeup haphazardly applied, smudged black liner and mascara, her thin frame busting out of a snug, bright red dress with a black lace shawl, trying to look sexy in a shredded up chair. I liked her, but she made me nervous.

She tilted her head and grinned, as though she were returning a flirtatious gesture. She had lipstick on her teeth.

"Hello, Ms. Wolfe."

"Oh, please don't call me that, Johny. It makes me feel like an old lady," she said slapping her hand down on the arm of the chair. "Call me Stella."

She took a cigarette out of a silver case and began packing it butt-side-down on the case before lighting it. She steadied a lit match to the end and took an elongated drag before releasing the smoke in one long, thick, lung obliterating exhale.

"Oh. Where are my manners? Cigarette, Johny?"

Opening the case again, she extended it over her lap and looked up at me — raising her eyebrows, as if to encourage me had I been shy to accept. She knew I didn't smoke but I had accepted her cigarettes a few times when I first started staying here, as a show of politeness. It didn't bother me to smoke here and there.

"No thanks, Stella. I'm good," I declined.

I took one of the LPs out, assessing its condition while attempting to put it on the gramophone. Stella watching me made me edgy, but I continued to fumble in an effort to hide it. Because she was silent, I looked back at her, and her eyes were hardly looking at me but hazily focused on a point on my back. She looked like this city, like a tall, smoky pillar in a concrete landscape, and she reminded me of Betty in that aspect. She ignored my staring at her while in her cloud for a moment, but I knew she saw me because her eyes widened and began to focus and move away.

"C'mon, Johny, one cigarette won't hurt. They're the good ones."

Feeling the push, I looked up at her, then down to the cigarettes. I hesitated. She wanted to win. She wanted me to walk towards her and accept her offer.

"Sure, why not? Thanks."

A silent minute passed until she remembered to hand me the matches. They were good cigarettes, brown with a gold shiny banner on the tip of the filter nearest the butt. I lit it exactly as she had. Smoke inside us, then into the air, and we repeated this until the room grew heavy with it. The cigarette would have tasted better if I was still accustom to smoking, but now it felt harsh on my throat. The concept of smoking always had a lure that surpassed the reality, just like so many other vices. Stella followed my exhalations, which I imagined to be purposeful, trying to let me know, if I hadn't picked up on it yet, that she was harmlessly playing with me.

"So, Johny, you want to play something on that old thing?" she asked, pointing to the gramophone.

"Yeah, I do, but I've never used one of those before. Do you mind if I put a record on now?"

"Yes, yes, yes! I already said so. Don't make me tell you ten times. Please, put one on. Nobody ever uses that thing and I put quite a bit of money into restoring it. It was my mother's and she was a great music lover."

It was evident that she was fighting to appear sober, and as she spoke her words came out increasingly slow and mumbled.

"Lots of old things in this house. I can't say what works and what doesn't. None of my kids want to lift a finger around here to clean up, and I have a bad back, so it's all collecting dust. Every once in a while we get a houseguest that cleans. Someone like you."

"Yeah" was all I could say. I was the houseguest she hoped would spiff up the joint next. A few times I had tidied up but the place could have used a lot more. It was the least I could do.

"Figure out how it works. I can't remember, but there's a knob on the side. Just put it on and move the needle to the record and it'll start. Play 'til your heart's content.' I'm sure you'll pick something I'll like." She flicked her cigarette in an ornate silver ashtray, and then passed it to me.

"I will. Thank you, Stella," I said, taking the ashtray from her.

I tried the record but it didn't work, and I didn't feel like asking her to show me because she looked so cozy in the chair now. I then retreated to the couch and read the back of a few albums, returning the ashtray to her, even though she seemed satisfied to flick her ashes right on the floor. When she saw I noticed, she let out a faint giggle and said the maid would take care of it. I never saw anything resembling a maid in the house and knew not to believe her. For an even longer moment we sat in silence. I looked out the dirty window and she watched me, shifting her eyes up and down my body. It was disconcerting, but I don't think she meant it to be. It felt more like a curious observation. She sipped her drink, taking bigger gulps each time the lipstick-stained tumbler rim met her lips. Every glass in the house had her lipstick stains on them, even after they were washed. Whatever that stuff was made of, it was waterproof, soap-proof, sponge-proof, everything-proof. All her makeup was. First thing in the morning it was still on.

"Whatcha doing walking dogs, Johny? Look at your Brando looks! You should be in the movies or something.

I feel like you could do so much more." All of a sudden, she came to life and adopted some sort of 1920's accent. And here I thought she was on the verge of passing out. She must be getting a second wind.

"Yeah," I replied, leaning forward, looking at my shoes. I tried to think of a real response, but couldn't. She leaned forward, too, meeting my eyes at the same level, looking as though she were anticipating an explanation. Something. Anything. Her interest was flattering and caustic at the same time.

"Coulda, shoulda, woulda," I said, shrugging. "I'm too —"

She cut me off. "No!" she started before I could finish. Her head was shaking side to side.

"Don't say that. You're not too old. You can do anything you want. I'm so tired of hearing young people use that as an excuse. There may be some things that are unrealistic at your age, but I started many adventures later in life that I succeeded in."

Just as I almost started to take her seriously, she completely lost me on the last part. I can't imagine what these things were that she succeeded in. As far as I could tell, she seemed like a woman who'd given in to constant indulgence and did nothing useful with her time. Then I suddenly questioned who I am to know or judge her success, her sobriety, her usefulness, her preferences, her status, or how she spends her time, etc. I didn't know anything about her life, or who she is, or was, or what she succeeded in, enough to say she had nothing or everything to speak of. She did what she wanted, and there was nothing wrong or immoral with her liberal ways.

"Sandra told me a little bit about you and what you've been through this year."

She continued talking, but I stopped listening. What and how much had Sandra relayed to her mother? It seems natural that she'd inquire about me, but I didn't want her knowing my history or circumstances. When I tuned in again, Stella was saying how, in spite of not appearing to be the perfect parent, she indeed asks about her children's acquaintances. She's looking out for them — and the house.

"All good people. All my kids attract good people. Their friends and lovers have brought color to our home. There's never been any trouble. I did a good job and I trust them and their choices."

I listened to what she was saying and understood she was smarter than she seemed to be, more deliberate, more watchful. By what standards she defined people as 'good' were unknown to me, but I actually believed there might be some truth to what she said. I liked her positivity, faith, and trust, something I lacked but was trying to attain. Finally, I began to see more of this woman and understand that there was more to her. The same went for the rest of the family.

A cat came in from the basement and started rolling on its back on the rug; a big, orange tabby that Sandra named Caesar. He mostly roamed the alleys behind the house, so when he came inside it was a special occasion. As Stella prattled on, and I tuned out, I saw him spray in the corner on the long drapes after sniffing around. She didn't hear or see, and I don't know it would have mattered if she had.

"Johny, Johny," she repeated, attempting to catch my gaze away from watching Caesar.

"You've had some hard times, must have taken a lot to sleep in the park. It's okay, we all have our tough times. God knows I have. But you are welcome here. It's a pleasure, truly. We all like you and hope you are at ease with us."

I couldn't believe Sandra told her. I was upset, though there was no reason to be. Perhaps this knowledge made me welcome in the house on account of her feeling sorry for me. I still carried so much shame in people knowing where I'd been. I thought they'd dislike me, distrust me, look down on me, but they didn't.

When she spoke she was more passionate than I'd ever known her to be. And, though I had avoided talking with her before, I was happy we got a chance to sit here together today. After all, I was living in her house, sleeping with her daughter in her daughters' bed. Paying little rent her way for this prime location. Despite my anxiety around her, I wanted to be real with her as she was real with me.

Caesar meowed up at her crossed legs from the foot of her chair. He watched her talk, waiting for the okay, which he finally got, leaping onto her lap. She stroked his neck and he started purring immediately, stretching his nose to meet hers. Then she stopped talking and sat looking down at the floor. Her head started to bob from side to side and her eyes rolled back every time she blinked, a long blink, taking a few seconds for her to lift her lids again. She came back for a moment.

"Oh, you beautiful big cat, Caesar."

He stood on her lap with his tail raised as she spoke to him. Speaking in a quiet voice now, drinking from her almost-empty glass one last time before setting it back on the table. Then, while still holding her cigarette, which was down to the filter and extinguished, her head slumped forward and she passed out. Caesar nestled on top of her slender thighs.

Outside the sky turned gray and it started to pour. The sound of the rain and Caesar's loud purring sent me into a euphoric state of pre-sleep dreaming, scattered images, where Sandra had come home and started touching me, but I couldn't keep my head up to look at her. I was drooling on myself, and every time my head bounced, my eyes, trying to focus, could see Stella watching me while continuing to smoke and drink. But she was out cold, probably for hours if not all night. She'd wake up with a sore neck and an even greater need to start the routine again, light herself a cigarette, pop a few pills, pour a glass, and watch her television series.

I drifted into another dream where I was floating above Manhattan. The great city was crumbling beneath me. Some realized it and others rushed about obliviously, as though they were blind to it. I could see their faces, like I had a moving camera running through the streets, and I could see this metallic light drenching their skin, and clothes, and lives, like the light that bounces off the tall buildings. I looked down, melancholic, while I watched people toppled by falling skyscrapers, others still scurrying about while on their phones, still not noticing a thing, as they were about to be next. And I knew I would miss this place and all these people when it finally turned to ruins.

"Goodbye, Blue York City," I said.

I woke to Sandra tapping my thigh.
"Hey, sleepyhead, come upstairs to bed."
I yawned and stretched my legs and arms.
"Where were you all this time?" I asked, my eyes trying to open. She kissed my lips.
"Long story." Following that, her eyes turned away from mine to her passed out mother in the chair.
"Crazy day. I'll tell you tomorrow."
As we mounted up the staircase, I began to wake, and noticed she looked different today and got some color. I shrugged it off and jumped in bed, stripping down to my boxers. I heard her brushing her teeth in the bathroom, before going downstairs. She was down there for a while. I wondered if Stella woke and if they were talking. Sandra returned in the room with Caesar in her arms, putting him on the bed and closing the door. He smelled like rain and

alleys, but he was soft, cute, and purring as loudly as before.

*****

"Oh, Jack, look who it is! It's Johny!"

Betty looked at me with Jack on her lap, holding him up on his hind legs and guiding his paw, as if he were waving to greet me. She had a big smile on her face and kept moving her eyes from Jack to me. His nub tail was wagging about, hitting her in the chest and moving her scarf. Betty was getting out in the sun every day, sometimes coming with Jack and me on walks in her chair. She was looking so much better and had been happy the past few weeks, always showing so much enthusiasm upon seeing me. She was the kind of person that opened more and more of herself the longer you knew her.

Jack liked me more than Betty and Harvey. And I know this because I was the only one who played with him like he needed. Jack was a hyperactive terrier, and that energy had to go somewhere. There were a few spots in the park where I would unleash him and we would run around. He'd chase me and bark while trying to nip my ankles. I, like Betty, hadn't been so happy in a long time. I had almost forgotten about the uncertainty of my future that used to bother me so much. I was able to finally suppress and ignore it, or release it, but every time I let the thoughts creep back, I got depressed. Betty wouldn't be around forever. Sandra and I might not always be together. I can't live at her house forever. Tony is unreliable and I haven't seen him in weeks. There will be another winter, and another after that, and after that, and I'm not getting any younger. What will I do when these things dissolve and I'm left with nothing and nobody? Oh well, I said to myself, oh well. It doesn't bother me anymore. It can't. Everything is going to be all right. Everything is always all right, somehow. And, if it isn't, I think I could still be happy anyway.

"Hey, little buddy, hey you! Come here, lil' guy! Ready for a walk?"

Betty let go of Jack and he ran to me. When I squatted down, he stood, his front legs on my knee, trying for his tongue to reach my face. Jack kept me going. I wish that he didn't live with a paralyzed lady in the middle of a metropolis, but in a suburb or rural area with active people, where he could be free. He had no choice in the matter, destined to be this woman's trusty companion. Every time I left he looked as though he wanted me to take him home, and I wanted that, too.

Today, Sandra and Bella are to finally meet Jack. We would link up in the park before lunch, but I was running late to meet them. Betty wanted me to sit and talk and I couldn't tell her I was in a rush, or that I had a play date for Jack. I didn't want to tell her yet, just in case she was uncomfortable about Jack playing with another dog. Most likely she wouldn't be, but now it was a matter of just getting out the door and not wanting to bring up anything that could stall me.

"Harvey isn't well," she started to say, her face assuming a solemn look.

"Last week he wasn't feeling well and this week I told him to take some time off and see a doctor. I reckon he's there now. Anyway, he's been off getting his strength back, just in case you were wondering where he was."

"What's the matter with him?" I noticed he wasn't there for a few days, but it wasn't that abnormal. He had taken a few long weekends before and I'd do a little extra for Betty.

"I hope everything is all right. Maybe it's just a bug going around," I offered.

"Course. He's a young, healthy man. I'm not even worried as I'm sure it's nothing," she said before wheeling back to her desk and putting her glasses on to begin reading.

There had been too much rain and humidity, mixed with cool nights. It was hot for October, an Indian summer. Even Sandra was complaining about not feeling well. My eyes fixed for a second on something she was holding, something I'd never noticed before, a tiny photo of someone in a tiny frame. She saw me look at it and quickly tucked it away in her chair. I was curious to know who it was — her deceased husband, her kids, her mother, maybe someone else? It was only recently that she had even told me about her kids, and that they were gone. I wanted to ask more, but as usual was too timid to bring up what may be a sore subject for her. What she told me about them wasn't substantial, only that they all lived in California and had families of their own, rarely having the time to return to the East Coast to see her. It was evident she didn't want to talk about them. There were no pictures of them anywhere that I could see. Maybe they came around on the holidays and I hadn't been around long enough to meet them.

In all these months working for her I had never seen or heard of any visitors, friends, family — nobody but Harvey and Jack. And it was only once that Harvey mentioned Phillip, Betty's late husband. Phillip had been ill for years before he passed. Harvey had originally been hired to assist him but Betty found Harvey such a comfort that she kept him on, and eventually he cared for her and became a vital part of her life who she completely trusted. I wondered if Harvey knew everything about Betty. She was a mystery to me, and it was hard to believe that anyone knew her private life and history.

Deep down I was jealous of Harvey and what he shared with Betty. She taught me so much, things I was only beginning to understand, and I wanted to be as indispensable to her as he was. I didn't care about her age;

I wanted to be there for her forever. I looked up to her in more ways than she knew. Perhaps she was used to it. Perhaps she liked keeping men around who adored her, like Stella does. Perhaps she loved us back, too.

"Well, I hope it's nothing at least." There was a pause after she said this.

"You know, Johny, when I look at you, I forget I'm old. I forget I'm feeling death stalking me. I forget I've nothing to look forward to anymore. I have children older than you, children that are busy with their own lives and families. And, when I remember my age, it feels like a cruel trick nature played on me. It feels unfair. I want my youth back. But you being here helps ease the blow of it all."

I didn't know what to say, but I understood. It was as though she read all my thoughts and suffered the same relentless frustrations that I do. There was nothing I could say, but I looked at her in agreement. The room got very small and she returned to her work, so I stood up to take Jack. I so badly wanted to say something to her. Later I would have my chance, but to say what, I had no idea. I wanted to say that being around her made me feel good, too. But I wouldn't.

As soon as I spotted Bella and Sandra waiting for me in the park, I forgot Betty's words that hung over me as I left. I forgot all the worries in the world. Bella tugged at the leash to reach me, jumping up on her hind legs, singing a song in howls and grunts to draw me near. I missed her so much. Sandra seemed unbothered by my lateness. She looked tan and vibrant, wearing a green and black summer dress that flowed down to just below her knees and fitted her perfectly, showing off every curve. I'd never seen her in this dress, but she had bought a bunch of similar ones a while back. Her eyes were a lighter shade of brown today in contrast with her skin. The trees behind her were starting to turn October colors and I was overcome at the sight of it all.

Her hair was tossed in a bun with loose spiral curls framing her face. I was so busy looking at her that I didn't notice the dogs sniffing each other. Jack was scared stiff and trying to be cool. Bella ran her nose all the way along his back and inspected his rear. We had them tight on their leashes as a precaution, but then Bella got down in a play position and started to whimper. Jack responded with equal submission. Success! They were instant friends, just as we'd hoped. When we reached a clearing, we took them off-leash. They chased each other in circles and played for an hour.

I reached for Sandra's hand and held it near to me. She locked my arm in hers. I'd never let myself feel like this before. And I was incapable of feeling this way before because I repressed myself for so long. I had to hold back from getting emotional. Sandra was my wife and Bella and Jack were our children. It was as perfect as any other family.

When Sandra and Bella walked away, I watched them from the bench with Jack until they faded into the trees. I didn't know what would become of us. Today I was willing to accept that there is such a thing as love in my life, and it came in many more forms than I had known it could.

No matter what the future held, I felt content in this moment. I wasn't afraid of getting old alone; being poor, being abandoned, being hurt. I didn't know or trust to what point I could keep letting go. I didn't know if tomorrow I would feel differently about everything or if I would still love Sandra, or if all the doubts would come back. But, at least for now, I knew peace, even if it was brief.

Happiness had entered my life slowly these past months, but I found it so foreign that I initially began rejecting it, going so far as to try sabotaging it on occasion, just as I'd always and unconsciously done. But now I was changing and I felt it. I pleaded with myself, 'Let this time be different. Don't ruin this. Don't hurt her.'

One thing was certain for both of us; to be alone at our ages was less than ideal; to both be living at her mom's was less than ideal; to both be established in nothing was less than ideal; to both be headed nowhere was less than ideal. We needed one another to ease these realities when they hit us hard, and to accept that these realities weren't really that bad, anyway.

I went to visit Tony after I left Betty's. I hadn't seen him in a few weeks and was thinking of him a lot lately. He wasn't one to keep up with texts so I thought he was just busy. I kept trying to call, but nothing, thinking he just didn't pay the bill. His phone had been disconnected for a week and now I was getting worried. I walked over to his place and used my key to enter. There was no sign of him. I sat on the couch for a half an hour, looking around and remembering my nights there. The place was a mess despite all the cleaning I had done when I lived there. In a short time he had dirtied it up again with his empty bottles, cigarette butts, and take-out food boxes. There was a pile of Styrofoam containers with rotting dried chicken wings and fried rice in the sink, but an empty trash bin a few feet away that he could have easily used instead. A guy who's barely here, and only to sleep and shower when he is, who could do all this is truly a talent. There was no rhyme or reason to his madness.

I thought of the last time I saw him and still had a distinct image of his sunken face in my mind. He looked disturbing, begging to borrow forty dollars. He pretended to ask about Sandra and how it was going, but his hands were unsteady the entire time, waiting for me to finish so that he could grab the money and be done with the formalities. It was then that I knew I couldn't return to living with him even if I barely saw him. I gave him the money out of pity. Before I was still sleeping at his place here and there, so as not to be living at Sandra's full time. Towards the end he was never there. We never drank together. No more late night/early morning conversations. I felt like I lost my only friend — one of the closest friends I'd had in a long time — and regretted leaving him like I did. Maybe if we were still close he wouldn't have spiraled down so low and I'd know where he was.

It hadn't affected me sooner because Sandra had all but replaced Tony and I didn't give him much thought, especially since he'd become so junked out. I told myself I'd see this place again, and I left ten dollars on his bed with a note, just in case he was back, so I could know next time I came if he'd been here and scooped it up. I wanted to know he was still alive. Damn, Tony. I always thought he was so cool for not giving a fuck, but now I wished he'd get his shit together. He deserved it. He deserved to be in Puerto Rico with his mom, living in a real home. But I knew he never would. This city would be the end of him. I regretted thinking it, but I prayed I was wrong.

I stopped by the hangout in the park and it was packed, yet no sign of Tony. Joey and the other guys asked me if I'd seen him even before I got a chance to ask them. Everyone was shocked that there was no news of him. Had he been arrested? Was he was in rehab? Was he in the hospital? Those were the only viable places he might be. If he were on the streets, he'd have made his rounds here by now. Someone would have seen him. Even if he was dead, and we didn't like to talk about it, somebody would have known. The word on the street travels fast.

No, Tony is fine. He mentioned a while back that one of these days he was going to check himself into a facility. That's where he's got to be right now. I chose not to think about it and returned to his place with a box of trash bags and cleaning supplies and got to work. Sandra texted me a few times asking where I was, but I didn't feel like answering her until late, then told her I was staying at Tony's, cleaning up. I told her he had disappeared and I wanted to get his place decent for when he came back. She didn't reply and I knew she missed me. All I wanted was to be alone. There was a lot I wanted to think about tonight, and a lot I didn't want to think about, too.

*****

"Any news from Harvey?" I asked.

"Strangely, no," Betty said. "I left a message with him yesterday. Perhaps he's been busy. He may have called. I need to check today's messages."

Betty and I had lunch in the dining room. She'd hired a chef to cook for her while Harvey was away, and they prepared quite a spread. Harvey usually picked up food from a restaurant or had it delivered. I told her about Jack meeting Bella the week before, and she was happy to hear it. She said she always wanted Jack to make friends. For the first time, because of the story of Bella and Jack, I told her about Sandra. I even used the word 'girlfriend.' I don't know why this was difficult for me, but it was. There was stillness in the air while talking about her, as though I had some obligation to Betty. I'm sure it was only on my side and she felt no such thing.

"Tell me about her, Johny. Does she love dogs like you do?"

"Yes. She loves all animals. But I'd say she loves cats the most."

"Very nice. How long have you two been together?"

"Not so long. Five months."

It was then that the phone rang. A woman from the kitchen came into the room and motioned that it was for Betty, so she wheeled over to the phone by the window to get the call. The conversation from afar looked like good news.

"Hello! Yes! I was worried about you. We've missed you here. Johny and I are having a late lunch. Tell me, now, what's the story? When are you coming back to us?"

But then a look of concern grew across her face as she listened, for what felt like a few minutes. She sat intently, her expression dropping, her eyes scanning the floor. She kept repeating "oh," "ok," "oh no" every here and there. It had to be Harvey. And the news, it turned out, didn't sound good. I didn't know whether I should ask immediately or wait for her to tell me.

When she hung up, she turned her chair and looked at me blankly for a few seconds. Her face instantly lost its glow.

"It was Harvey?"

She nodded, her face unchanged.

Eventually she spoke: "It's not good, Johny. The doctor says he doesn't have much…"

It was then that her voice began trembling and her lips began quivering. A few times she tried to finish the sentence, but she couldn't until she regained composure. Her hands looked fragile as they scrambled to clench the arms of her chair. There was nothing I could say. She knew I understood and didn't bother trying to finish, because she couldn't. All I could do was look down at the beautiful plate of food. I immediately lost my appetite. I really liked Harvey and was in shock, and still wanted to know the details but refrained from asking. We sat in silence for an hour before departing and she tried to keep herself together while finishing her meal, then let me accompany her up to the study. I don't know how she could even eat. I don't think she knew how either, but I'm sure she did it because she had to preserve the little will she had left to survive.

"Please, Sandra, just hold me."
"I'm so sorry, baby. So sorry."
Sandra sat on the bed while I rested my head on her lap. I was devastated about Harvey and worried what this would mean for me. Could I replace him? In a way I wanted to — it was a relief, if she'd let me, —but I don't think that would happen. There wasn't enough time to start over again. Betty would never love me the way she loved Harvey. The thought of losing my comfortable position there also had me in knots. I could never tell Sandra this. I was aware of how sick it would all sound, that I wanted so badly to be close to Betty, so I kept it in. If she knew Betty she might understand how it was possible to feel like I do.

"And to top it all off, Tony's still missing. I don't know what to think anymore. I'm just so lucky I have you. You know, Sandra, that day when I saw you standing in the park with Bella, I was in disbelief at how beautiful you looked, with your hair up and the pretty dress. I keep thinking of it. It scared me. I love you so much."

The words came out with no forethought. They were completely natural and I was as taken aback as she appeared to be. She cradled my face and drew it towards her stomach.

"I love you so much, too, you have no idea. That day was perfect. I felt the same way, Johny. I never thought I'd meet someone like you. I thought I'd always be alone and nobody would ever love or understand me. Nobody ever has. And then I found you."

"Exactly. I always felt the same. We found each other."

We kissed and made love that night. I was terrified by it all, as usual, but it was okay.

*****

I continued returning to Tony's and always saw the same ten dollars I left on his bed. I continued to stop by the park and ask around for him. Nothing. I continued to believe he was still out there somewhere, dealing with what he had to do. And I continued going to Betty's to care for Jack, watching her decline a little bit more each day. She hired a nurse named Michelle, who was probably a good nurse but treated Betty like a child. Most the time Michelle was paging through magazines on the couch and reminding Betty of her next med times. She would once in a while wheel the oxygen tank in the room, instructing Betty to take a few puffs when she sounded wheezy.

Michelle was attractive for a middle-aged woman. She never ate with Betty and me, always brought her own meals in Tupperware containers. Everything looked healthy, like fancy bird fare. Her skin was light black, mulatto looking, and she had a Jewish last name: Stein. She must be from Brooklyn.

The updates on Harvey were constant. Betty became obsessed with talking to him on the phone and relaying every detail of their conversation to me as though it were all she had left. He had a rare type of cancer that was rapidly overtaking him. Betty kept insisting that she visit him, but he kept refusing, saying that he couldn't let her see him like this, not yet at least. I think she reserved some hope that maybe he would pull through, and likely he knew this. She was paying for all his medical care and insisted he see her doctor, one of the best in the city, so she claimed.

I talked to him on the phone a few times and wasn't sure what to say. His voice sounded so bad that I was unable to say anything genuine. The room was always quiet for what felt like an hour when Betty got off the phone with him. There was nothing upbeat to say to break the silence. It had to happen naturally. We had to forget enough to go on. Even Michelle knew this and kept silent.

Later one Sunday, I was about to leave when Harvey walked in the study with his wife, a beautiful woman with blond hair. Betty and I looked at him in shock as he entered, seeming pleased to see us, as if nothing had happened, as if it were a regular day. He was barely recognizable, and it was difficult to hide my surprise at how thin he had become.

He kissed Betty on both cheeks and she let out an, "Oh dear lord," to which he only laughed. I got up and shook his hand and gave him a hug. We all sat and he introduced me to his wife, Nicole. Conversation started slow, but it eventually led to the obvious.

"Harvey, tell me, how is Dr. Page treating you? He was always very good to me, one of the best. If anyone can help, it is he."

"Yes. Nicole and I wanted to thank you again for referring him to us. He is great. There are no guarantees, but he said he's trying everything he can. The chemo was hard but I'm feeling positive. We've been reading up about everything, from natural cures to retreats, everything."

He said this while clasping Nicole's hand tightly in his lap.

"That warms my heart more than you know," Betty said. "Well, we anticipate your return. By the way, this is my nurse Michelle. She's been taking care of me."

Michelle came from the back of the room, walking towards Harvey to shake his hand. She seemed uneasy, but friendlier with him than I'd ever seen her to be with me. I got distracted from the conversation, watching her as she sat closer to our circle on the couch. She watched Harvey as he spoke with Betty about feeling better these last few days. I was trying to make sense of it when I heard Harvey mention his kids, which caught my attention. As I tuned in to the conversation, I wondered how it was that I knew so little about him. He said something about his adult son from a previous marriage trying to come over from Ireland to stay with him, but how he was running into problems. I kept trying to listen, but Jack was crying at Harvey's ankles for attention the entire time. I was annoyed that Harvey didn't notice Jack or make an effort to touch him at all. There was a moment of silence, then Betty looked at Harvey and said, "Let's speak of it on the phone tomorrow. I'd like to help."

I was petrified to look at him because I was reminded of my own mortality. He was gray, his hair had fallen out, and his skin was patchy, scaly, and pallid. Far from the handsome man I had met earlier this year. At one point, Nicole and Harvey agreed to stay for dinner, until Harvey started to feel sick. Nicole took charge and guided him out, rushing our goodbyes and disappearing out the door in a flash. Betty and I exchanged glances, confused and disappointed, like we got left hanging.

I felt that I was becoming much of what Harvey had been to Betty; someone who started working for her and ended up spending most of his time hanging around her house as a companion. Michelle started to become one of us, too, another fixture in Betty's world. We were her social life, her family, her everything. She would provide anything I needed just to stay with her, but she would be gone soon, and then what? How would I begin again? Would I go groveling back to Chris and Lee? I needed Betty and hoped she needed me, too, in every way. She drew me in ever since I first heard her voice on the phone, ever since I saw the photograph of her on my first day, and more and more every day since then.

But I didn't have to think about what would happen to Betty and me after Harvey. A decision was made. And it was as much a surprise as it was liberation. A week after

Harvey's visit I went to walk Jack, and Betty was sitting in her study as usual, peering out onto the city through her great big windows. It was raining again, but not enough to interfere with a stroll. She didn't turn to greet me and I knew something was wrong. I had a feeling what it was as soon as I saw Michelle in the foyer downstairs. She gave me a long faced look as I entered and just shook her head when I asked how Betty was doing. Harvey had died earlier that morning. I knew it.

Jack was on Betty's lap and she held him firmly as he tried to escape and run to me, but she wouldn't let him go. I sat on the couch facing the opposite wall, looking at the large painting with the gentlemen and their dogs, as Betty often would while thinking of something. I saw her from the back and remarked in my mind how feeble she looked. She turned half way around so I could see her. Her profile was how it always was, bathed in light with her translucent skin, eyes red and glossy with tears she didn't bother to wipe away. The gray beast of a city was beyond her; her empire had fallen. After 5 minutes she turned completely around to face me and started to speak. It evidently took all her energy to get the words out clear and strong.

"It's funny, Johny. We all have so much hurt, and we keep passing it on like a disease, from one to the next, to the next. If only we knew better, we could avoid so much of it. If only I knew better. I'm tired of all this regret and pain I harbor. I've had enough."

I couldn't think of one word to say. Nothing was expected. As always, I understood her.

"And here I thought maybe I wouldn't die alone. After watching everyone else die before me, I hoped someone could watch me go and hold my hand. I long for the comfort of someone who I can be close to. Everyone in my life has left me. But here I am, I'm not afraid anymore, and I can't hold this poor creature captive to this life. I need to move on."

She started to lose herself crying and it was hard for me to watch. I wanted to be by her side but I knew not to run to her.

"Please, Johny, take him," she said, holding Jack up on her lap with all her strength. "Please give him a better life. There is a check for you in an envelope downstairs on the table. I want you and Sandra to give him all the love you can. You two are the best people I know. I trust your heart is pure and you'll give him the life he deserves."

I was in shock. Betty was relieving me, letting me go, asking me to take little Jack and a severance check and leave so she can face her fears and be alone. My instinct was to talk her out of it. I started to ask her if she was sure, but she kept repeating that she'd made her decision. It was her only wish. Betty was not the type to change her mind or give in. After a minute, I knew I had to do it. And, more importantly, I knew this was what she had to do.

I rose to walk towards her and scoop Jack off her lap, but fell to my knees beside her chair, sobbing and holding her hand. My entire body was shaking. She cupped her bony hands over mine, releasing Jack, who then sat beside me. I didn't think I would ever lift my head to meet her eyes, but I did. It was the only moment, the last moment, I could tell her something before I left, and I knew I would never see her again.

"Thank you," I said. "I love you."

I felt no surprise from her, as though she always knew. As though she felt the same way.

"Yes, my beautiful, beautiful boy. Me too."

I was okay with that. That was as much as she could give, and it meant everything to me.

When I calmed down enough to stand and grab Jack's leash by the couch, I looked to her and hesitated, but she'd returned to her place before the window peering out onto the rainy park. Her body caved forward as she seemingly tried to stop herself from screaming out in agony. In an attempt to save her pride in this moment, she lifted her arm and motioned for me to finally let her go. It was time. I left her home and never saw her again.

On the way out, I took a long look at the picture of her I so loved, against the city, young and beautiful, and blue. She was always so blue. She reminded me of clean glass, tall windows, skyscrapers, freckles, geometric shapes, rain, black, white, blue, gray, and clear skies with fluffy white clouds.

Michelle came over to me at the door and gave me a hug. Here she was, prepared to act as the next companion for Betty through to her death. It was ironic that it would be she, someone who Betty had little connection with. For what reason Betty's children left her I can't begin to fathom, but it was rotten of them.

I spent the remainder of the afternoon walking Jack to Tony's to check one more time. No sign of him. He's in Puerto Rico with his mother. I kept repeating this in my mind and picturing him in paradise, helping his mother care for the animals and picking fruit off trees. Then I walked home with Jack and waited for Sandra. Luckily nobody was around. Better that Sandra explain the situation to her mom than I do. Jack was so happy to be with me, like he knew now he was free, like he got his wish. I felt this was my purpose, to be here for this dog, to give him another life, and to help free Betty.

It was meant to be exactly like this, as some strange destiny for us all. Like puzzle pieces fitting together, like a design.

Jack and I took a nap in Sandra's bed. He just wanted to curl under my arm. The adrenaline and emotion of the day took everything out of me. I never looked at the check that Betty left me. That would be for another day. I wasn't ready for that. She was already gone to me, another ending, and it cut me deeply, more than anything I'd ever experienced or thought I could feel. I think what hurt most is that I knew she was dying, that I couldn't help her, that I couldn't offer her anything, and that I couldn't have more time with her, not even one more day. There was nothing I could do. Except take Jack.

Everything was going to have the same outcome no matter what. There was no real way of being sure of anything, or knowing better, as Betty put it. I wanted to return to something familiar, but had no idea what that was. I just needed a break. I felt reminded of how Betty must have suffered with such loneliness for so long. I have Sandra now. She will be home soon.

Then, an idea surfaced. I decided to go see my mother. It had to be done. I needed to start over and make amends. I did not want to neglect her as Betty's children neglected her.

*****

"You're leaving? Why? Honey, you can't just leave Jack all of a sudden after bringing him here. I can't believe you could leave him at all. You've wanted him for so long and now he is here and you leave? When are you coming back?"

Sandra had so many questions. I knew she'd take my news hard.

"Baby, I just gotta figure out some stuff. Please give me time. I haven't seen my mom in years and I can't say how long I'll be there, but you know I'll be back. Jack will be fine. I'm no good to either of you right now until I get through this."

"I understand that. I just want to have an idea how long you're going so I can prepare to take care of Jack. I hope you're coming back. If it's me just be honest and tell me."

"I don't know how you equate my going away to figure things out and see my mom to leaving you, but that's not what's happening here. I'd tell you rather than using a cowardly excuse. I wish you'd understand. So much has happened. Tony is gone, Harvey is dead, and Betty is dying. I have no job. I just want to get out of the city and breathe and it has nothing to do with you. I'm so stressed, and I don't want to get depressed on top of that. And, no, I don't know when I'll be back because I don't know how long it will take. I need to have a plan when I return."

I invited her to come but I knew she couldn't get work off. It was better she didn't. I even tried to find out if I could bring Jack but no bus would accept animals on board.

She came over and hugged me and I knew she wanted to cry, as did I. Her fear of rejection told her that I might not be back, which has probably happened to her before. I didn't know how to ask her to wait for me.

"It's really not a big deal Sandra. Please, trust me, I'll be back. I love you. You're the only one for me in the world."

She looked at me with tears in her eyes, saying nothing. She was really trying to change her ways, be calmer, and not act insecure and paranoid, as she had done in the beginning, which was turning me away. All she could do was wait, and I knew she loved me, so I hoped she would wait no matter how long it took to figure things out. Sandra is everything to me. If only she believed it. Nothing will change my mind about her, and she will see that when I come back and make a life for us both.

I packed a duffle bag full of essentials and headed to Penn Station under a peach November sky. Before I left I gave Sandra and Jack the biggest hugs I could and it broke me to walk out the door and turn away from them. The city all of a sudden looked new to me now that I was leaving. I had a fleeting thought that I could have done so much here, much more than I did. But I took it for granted and wallowed in it. 'So much time wasted,' I thought. 'What can I do now?' There is no getting the past back.

Airports, bus terminals, and train stations have always had an energetic appeal to me. The buzz of people who are coming and going, and their stories. It made me regret not traveling in my life, but I was excited to board the bus home, see my mother, and walk through the old neighborhood after all these years that I've been away.

I saw the city come to pass through the bus windows, and watch the Empire State Building fade into the projects of Pelham Bay. Goodbye, Blue York City. It has been years since I left. I once thought I would be stuck here forever, but now in hindsight I realize that it all wasn't so bad. It was a dream.

It was a short ride to a far-away place. I fell asleep thinking of Sandra and Jack. I missed her the second I left. Thoughts kept popping up in my mind, but not just of Sandra, of Betty, too. Maybe she was on her deathbed right now with a broken heart. Or maybe she would live on for years to come, find some fresh companionship, and have her children return to her, or find happiness alone. I had no idea and would never know. I continued to wonder about something I'd always been curious about, but never remembered to ask: who referred me to her? And what was the story behind the photo of her that she'd wanted to share with me?

When I spoke to my mom yesterday she was beside herself that I was coming home. It only just hit me now how much I was looking forward to it, too. My motivation for this visit was unclear to me. There was nothing else I could think of doing, nowhere else I could think of going, and nobody else I could think of seeing or wanted to see more than her. I just had to get up and go. Part of me did it because of Tony. Because he spoke of his mother so often and it made me cherish mine more. The other part of me did it for Betty. I didn't want to regret any more in my life that could be avoided.

I arrived in Boston, took another bus south, then a taxi directly to her house. As I walked towards my childhood home, I felt overwhelmed, haunted by this place that I almost, and tried, to forget. My mom grasped my face in her hands when she opened the door, like I was still a boy, kissing me on my cheeks and then hugging me with all her might. At that moment I knew I made the right decision visiting her. It felt like a greater force led me here — beyond knowingly wanting to see her. Something in me, something wiser, knew I needed to see what I ran away from. And I knew she needed to see me, too.

We walked into the house, a first floor apartment in an old, worn out triple-decker in a humble New England town south of Boston. The smell was the same, musty and stuffy, old furniture, old fabrics, old closets with the smells of mothballs. The odor from the gas being used for heat reminded me of the apartment in Crown Heights. The colors were the same, drab and faded brown and orange, seventies patterns decorating the drapes and wallpaper. I'm almost positive they were the same drapes, same wallpaper, same everything from when I was a kid. Half was strangely recognizable and the other half I couldn't be sure of. It was like I never left.

As always, the place was spotless, the pride of a working-class woman who was afforded few breaks in this life. A passing thought entered my mind: if I had a sister or a brother, or both, how different might this place be? Would there be cards on the fridge? Would there be grandchildren? Would it be like Sandra's family? Would my mom have been alone here all this time? I wish I weren't the only one for her.

I felt awkward walking in and sitting down, unsure if I should feel at home or like a guest. She kept grinning and asking me superficial questions about my life, as to which I didn't care to answer in depth because it had been a long day traveling. The air between us grew more and more stifled. I soon became weary with this interrogation, with her overeager efforts to force conversation as I was struggling to overcome my growing culture shock at being back. I summed things up in a few short sentences: Sandra is my girlfriend, I live in an apartment with her, I have a full-time job walking dogs, and that is all. I didn't talk of Betty, or living at Sandra's with her crazy family, or of anything else that might be complicated and time consuming to explain. I don't know if she would understand.

At her age, it's better to not know what you've missed in life, to not know what you never knew, where you've never been, to not know that the world is beyond what you ever thought possible. Her youth is long gone. She is provincial, sheltered in this small town. It made her seem naïve to me. I know she is not a jealous or envious person, but I didn't want to tell her anything that might make her feel that she didn't get out enough in life.

A timer went off in the kitchen. She paused our talk and walked over to the oven. She went on about how the neighborhood had changed, but I couldn't have cared less about the uninteresting people in this sleepy community. She failed to pick up on my disinterest, maybe because I was pretending to listen, so she went on, relaying local gossip. Holding a pan of roast chicken and potatoes, fragrant steam escaping the lid, with mitted hands she set our home cooked dinner down on the table.

I couldn't help judging her, but felt guilty again. I couldn't meet her eyes as she spoke. I cannot assume she didn't sense it, as she may have, but I didn't care. This was exactly how it was when I was a kid, when I left — everything she did seemed to annoy me because nothing ever changed. It was always the same gossip, the same food, the same everything.

"Mom, I don't want to eat that. I thought I told you that on the phone, no meat and potatoes. I asked for some pasta or pizza."

"Oh, Johny, I thought you were joking," she replied, looking deflated.

"No. Jesus, mom, why don't you listen to me? I don't want that. Now I gotta go back out and find some food."

I grimaced looking at it. Funny, because I still ate meat. When Sandra wasn't around I would have a burger or some fish, but it wasn't that often anymore. At this moment, looking at the chicken, I felt differently. I was done with it.

I was upset she made this dish because it was so predictable. It was the same dish she always made for my dad and me, and even after he left she persisted. There was no creativity to her cooking. My dad had grown tired of it, asked for something different, but she kept making it, like she didn't know how to cook anything else. She just didn't listen. I was upset she was so stubborn. And I was upset because it reiterated to me that she never changed, or tried to, or could fulfill a simple request for something new.

It was suddenly hard to sit still. I was bored in this house with her and hated myself for feeling like I did. I waited too long to come home and see her. Although I love her, I saw her as a stranger. My stomach ached with hunger, and everything about this setting made me want to run. I got up to go for a walk and process how I could feel at home with her, and how I could try to fight this urge to return to the city.

But she spoke, with words that sat me back in my chair. Looking serious, she took a seat and threw her arms up, staring at the door ahead.

"Oh, Johny, I'm trying. You don't want to eat this? Okay, I'm sorry. I'm sorry it made you so miserable and that you have a look of disgust on your face, that you hate this town and coming back. But it's just the two of us. Don't you see? We have to make this work. You are my son, my only child, and I am your only mother whether you like it or not. I am not sophisticated and I don't pretend to be, Johny, but you'll regret behaving this way one day, and I don't want you to. I won't let you. I want you to understand this right now: there is no use in it. This is as good as it gets."

Her words shot through my heart. I was speechless, tears streaming down my cheeks. She'd seen straight through me and was absolutely right. She always felt me judging her and holding back, yet said nothing. What a stunted adolescent I still am; and it seeps into every thought I have and every action I take. It is I who is small-minded and insecure, so offended by this place where mediocrity is freely displayed and accepted.

Even without ever leaving this town she knew the same things as someone who had, it made no difference. From her world here, standing in this same spot that she had called 'home' for all these years, she knew. She had an inkling the whole time, as did I, and as I would have if I never left. She always hid her sadness with a happy face, until now, and it's made me realize what a fool I'd been to dismiss her feelings just because she didn't, and couldn't, show them.

Her head was down and my eyes were closed. She got up and came near me. I felt her place her hand on top of mine on the table. She was standing behind me and pressing my tears away with her fingers. I abandoned her, just like my father had. Just like I abandoned everyone.

"I'm so sorry, Mom. I love you. I really didn't mean to be a jerk. I don't know what's wrong with me, truly. I want to be here with you. It's been a long day and I'm not in a good way. I'm sorry."

I couldn't recall the last time I spoke to her with sincerity. It was always a reaction, a response. Yes, I love her, as simple and real as she is. And, like she said, there isn't enough time. We are getting old and she knew it. She saw it on my face as I saw it on hers.

What a heart she has. That's all I could think. What a heart this sweet, patient, forgiving woman has, and how beautiful she is. I was a fool not to see it before.

I got up and gave her a hug as she cried, her head against my chest, looking like a little girl. As with everything, the emotion eventually subsided and we emerged out the other side. She wanted to apologize, but I wouldn't let her. She was right and she didn't have to be afraid I would walk out on her for it.

We decided to go out for dinner and I insisted on paying, though she tried to stop me. This time we started over. I opened up to her about my life as of this year; about Sara and the eviction, Tony, Sandra's house, Betty, Jack, and Chris and Lee. She smiled, cried, and laughed listening to my stories. I was glad to share them with her. I had never opened up to anyone in such detail, not even Sandra. It hurt my mom so deeply to hear about my homelessness. I never thought about how that would make her feel.

She kept asking about Betty. It was difficult to tell all the gritty details, because I couldn't easily mention Harvey or the last time I saw Betty. It was too fresh. It was difficult to even talk about Sandra. The more my mother learned of Betty, the more she expressed sorrow for her. It had never occurred to me how isolated Betty had been, and how my mother could understand that so quickly from my talking of her, despite their drastically different backgrounds. At the end of the meal she said she hoped to meet Sandra someday, that she could imagine the house we lived in with the eccentric Stella. I hoped she could meet them all, too. I didn't know how things would be when I returned, didn't know if anything would be the same. I looked up and said, "Of course you will, Ma."

Later that night I walked around the neighborhood alone. Things had changed in ways. Different faces on the same townies, more crime, poverty, immigrants, and drugs. It definitely wasn't the same place I grew up in. I would put my time into this visit, five days, maybe more. I would try to stay longer but I doubted it would be more than a week. There simply was nothing to do here and I was already desperate to find ways to pass the hours. I didn't know the next time I would be back this way, but I vowed soon, and next time I'd bring Sandra and Jack.

We ate together every night when she returned from work at the diner. I cooked for her and afterwards we watched her favorite shows. It was like clockwork, as though no time had gone by, exactly how I remembered it. She always smiled when she saw me. I wondered if anyone else had ever made her this happy. In all this time, did she ever meet anyone? Had she felt love from any man?

I studied her while she watched her shows sitting on the couch. The skin around her eyes had changed, hollow and red. Her hair was brown, but gray had taken over, and it was frizzy, kinky, and shaggily rested on her shoulders. The deep wrinkles that had set in all over her face; the nose with enlarged pores and tiny veins in her cheeks; the weight collecting around her neck and body like a big apple. Her waitress uniform from the diner where she worked was too tight, revealing her round midsection. It was ripped in places, but carefully stitched back together to conceal its overuse. She would laugh at something on the TV and, when her face fell back, her sagging cheeks formed engraved lines reaching from her nostrils to the corners of her mouth. Her stained teeth didn't do her any favors. On top of that, her discolored gums were worse than I remembered. I can't recall what she looked like when she was younger, if she ever was.

Stella had aged more gracefully than my mother. It was like night and day. If they were in a painting together, they would look like nobility and peasant, my mother being the latter. I wondered what Mom could have been if she was fit and had her hair done, if she had nice clothes, if she had regular facials and wore a little make up. Maybe she wasn't too old or too far-gone to find a guy that would love and care for her. But, despite her generous heart, no men showed interest in her, and she never got out there to meet any. I don't know if she gave up or lost feeling.

It rained on and off the entire six days I was there, at least once a day, remaining gloomy the rest of the time. I thought of New York, but it was a different gloom there, shiny compared to the dread of this place.

I thought of the view out Betty's windows and longed to be back. Back with a different start this time, though I didn't need to return just yet. The memory of it was inside me. When the day came to leave, I packed my duffle bag and took a long look around my room after making the bed. It was the same as I left it. Perhaps it would be the same next time I come.

Mom stood near the door with a brown bag lunch she packed for my journey. It was hard for both of us, but I hugged her for a whole minute and couldn't pull away until I knew I could keep the tears in. I kept telling her that I'd be back soon, that I would call her regularly, that I would even buy her a bus ticket to come visit Sandra and I. She showed enthusiasm, but I don't know if she believed it. I would make it happen and show her.

"Please, Johny, just be safe and take care of yourself. I don't want anything bad happening to my son."

For hours I sat across the street from the bus station on the curb, watching the buses depart to NYC without me. I couldn't board. I had to move forward in some other way to some other place. Ahead of me was a road going nowhere and I just kept walking and walking. I've been adrift my whole life and now I need to search for what it is I've been missing. Everything this past year has prepared me for this moment.

As I walked down the street with my duffle, I thought of my mother, the sight of her face as she hugged me again and again then bid me farewell from the doorway. The picture of her standing there, blowing me kisses with tears running down her face, would be branded on my brain forever.

Goodbye, Mother. Goodbye, for I've only just begun to know you. Goodbye to all that you could and couldn't teach me. You, Mother, and your routine, and your old curtains, odors of the kitchen and diner coffee on you, all the gorgeous rags you wear, your old wallpaper and your quiet life, your meat and potatoes, your game shows, and your loneliness. Love, your only son, Johny.

I thought about what the city had done to me. I thought about all that I had left behind for the time being. I thought about the dogs. I let it all go because it was all I could do. I would go back, when the time is right.

And I moved forward feeling that I might be nothing, and that I might be everything. It was a thing of freedom.

Made in the USA
Columbia, SC
27 June 2018